CATHY SHOUSE

HER BILLIONAIRE COWBOY'S
Pretend Proposal

GALLOWAY SONS FARM
A FAIR CREEK ROMANCE

HER BILLIONAIRE

COWBOY'S

Pretend Proposal

★ ★ ★

GALLOWAY SONS FARM
A FAIR CREEK ROMANCE

CATHY SHOUSE

Her Billionaire Cowboy's Pretend Proposal

GALLOWAY SONS FARM

A FAIR CREEK ROMANCE

CATHY SHOUSE

Her Billionaire Cowboy's Pretend Proposal
Cathy Shouse

Cover art by Blue Water Books

Contents

Get Free Books

Get free books, exclusive bonus content, and news of releases and sales by signing up for Cathy's newsletter. So join today.

Chapter One

Finn Moore stared out the window of her bookstore at the overcast sky, longing for sunshine—even just one ray. It'd been cloudy in Fair Creek for days, which wasn't helping with her mood or with bringing in customers, either.

She walked over to her display of children's books and rearranged a series about a cartoon dog so the Easter title faced out. Admiring her basket of blue artificial grass with tiny plastic books for reading in the tub, she decided it looked even better on the shelf than in the magazine that inspired it. When "Here Comes Peter Cottontail" played from her speaker in the corner, she hummed along.

But by the time she got to "hippity hoppity Easter's on its way," she turned off the music, trying to swallow the lump in her throat. She'd always avoided children's books to ease the ache in her heart, which hadn't worked. So this year she'd decided to push through and give children's merchandise a go.

"Are you ready for me to help with putting up your bunny, Finn?" Jessica Patterson, her best friend and business partner, stood in the attached bakery. "I've put the scones in so we should have time."

Finn had moved Wind in the Willows bookstore into the

building Jessica owned for The Sweet Shop Bakery two months ago. Jessica's latest food infatuation was scones, a delicious, dense biscuit-thing from the British baking show she'd binge-watched.

Finn stood back and admired the nice little book area she'd created, since many of her books weren't shelved yet. "That sounds great." Finn pulled the huge stuffed bunny out from under the counter and Jessica joined her as they headed outside. On the way, she did a lookover of the plants she'd put in the little separate entry.

Once outside, Finn flopped the rabbit onto the sidewalk and Jessica pulled long twist ties from her jeans pocket. After securing the tan bunny in a blue coat to the old-fashioned street pole in front of their businesses, Finn stepped back and admired its over-sized ears that pointed straight up. When she'd spotted him in the store, he'd made her smile from ear to ear, which was saying something.

Drizzle started coming down, although a bit of morning sun shone through. Great.

Jessica draped her arm over Finn's shoulder. "You okay? I know this can be a rough time."

She nodded. "It's hard to believe this month makes nineteen years. Let's not talk about it, okay? How do you like Peter? Money's tight, but I couldn't resist."

Jessica went over and arranged the carrot he was holding. "Maybe a bunny'll bring more people in. We need all the customers we can get."

A gust of wind rattled the awning material hanging over the mom-and-pop shops along Main Street, interrupting the stillness. Finn's hair swirled around her face, and she tried to tame it.

Jessica trapped her apron down with both hands while her blonde, curly ponytail whipped around. "Easter's just weeks away, though. Where'll he live after that?" The wrapper that enticed Finn to spend money she didn't have had guaranteed the stuffed animal's materials would hold up in any weather. It had better.

The wind died down. A golf cart rolled up the street. Ted and

Elizabeth Mitchell, a gray-haired couple who had both lost their spouses and tied the knot last year, exchanged waves as they went by.

Jessica grinned, her light coloring showing flushed cheeks. "The men's coffee group let women in this year, just for Elizabeth. Isn't love grand?"

Finn felt sure Jessica wanted to meet someone, although she hadn't dated anyone seriously.

Finn was the one who'd given up on the white picket fence and all the rest. "I wouldn't know if it is. I'll bring him in by the children's books."

"Didn't know kids' books were your thing."

True that. But breaking up with her boyfriend and not renewing her store lease in the city weren't in her plans, either.

"When I ended things with Brandon, I beefed up the children's book area." Her romance stories she'd always loved had started making her sad. Maybe seeing children in her store would fill the hole in her heart from missing Emily, the baby she'd given up for adoption.

"Oh, hon. I know being around kids has been rough, too."

Finn sighed and reached for the bunny's fur, which felt soft in her fingers. She and Jessica were chosen family, except her friend was more outgoing and sometimes promoted her opinions to a fault. Jessica's insistence on Finn staying with Jessica's grandma out-of-state when Finn was pregnant at 17 had cemented their friendship for life, though.

As different as their personalities were, they were sisters of the heart. Time to lighten her tone. "Just trying to figure out what sells in a little town."

"Aren't we all? Hey, with the wind died down, let's head in since the plants won't blow away when we open the door." Finn started toward the door to go inside, and Jessica followed. Once past the plant zone, Jessica made a beeline back toward her ovens. "Whoops! Fresh blueberry scones coming right up."

The sign hanging from the door flipped easily as Finn moved

it to "open," not like her electronic sign that sometimes glitched at her former store. Life really was simpler here, and cheaper, too. Maybe she would get onto it and stop missing the hustle and bustle she'd been used to.

Her gaze flitted around her space, its brick walls adding a vintage feel to the wooden, uneven floors. That's how she'd put a spin on it to her former bookstore customers in the city, anyway. Neglecting to tell them one wall of her small-town store had nearly caved in since the tornado had blown through had seemed smart.

Standing over where her oversized stock of leftover romance books surrounded her, heaped up in boxes, she sighed and held back a groan. Only yesterday she'd shoved them all next to walls after being strewn everywhere for the past two months since she'd moved in. A book on top featured a couple with their arms around one another and she nudged the box with the toe of her tennis shoe.

Jessica swooped over with one of her many bright, multi-colored plates that held scones and cinnamon rolls, which she balanced on one hand. Finn automatically leaned into her side of the space, where she'd gone for more muted tones.

"Hey, there's room for these on the shelves. And why's that over there?" Jessica dipped her head toward the sign labeled "romance fiction," stashed in a corner.

Finn shook her head. "My romance phase is behind me. I wouldn't want to lead my customers on."

Jessica rolled her eyes. "That's crazy. I went to the signings you hosted for authors—amazing events..." She let her voice trail off. "This doesn't have anything to do with B, does it? Trust me, you just haven't met the right one."

Jessica couldn't even bring herself to say Finn's ex's name. She was sweet to stick up for her. Finn decided to state the obvious. "Living in a small town like this is going to reduce the pool of eligible men and lower our chances." Not that Finn cared.

She tapped her chin, as if she hadn't thought all of this

through, hadn't been awake nights wrestling with it either. "Maybe I'll expand into YA and draw in the older kids and some adults that way."

Jessica stomped her foot in her bright green plastic clog the shade of artificial Easter grass. Gaudy was the new black with her. "That's like me deciding not to sell cinnamon rolls. Gotta bake what people want, especially in a small town."

"Let's see what happens. I can always shift strategies." They stood waiting, neither sure what to say. But Finn did have to pay attention to her profits. Her gaze was drawn to the far wall that needed to be repaired and tried not to think about more expensive maintenance needs that had been put off for too long either. Getting condemned might be on the table if she couldn't pay her part.

A tiny thread of guilt registered in Finn's gut. She came back to Fair Creek partly to stick it to the landlord for skyrocketing her lease rate. The old amount had already been a struggle to meet and landed her in debt. Her obligations were less in Fair Creek. Paying rent to Jessica for the store and the upstairs apartment, which would help her out, mattered though. She couldn't afford to drop books that might bring her bigger profits.

So, there was that.

As if reading her thoughts, Jessica shoved the plate under her nose. "Here. Have a scone. I need to get moving."

She grinned. "Thought you'd never ask." The doughy bread with blueberries warmed her fingers and promised the ultimate in comfort food. One tasty bite opened up a world of possibilities, as her mind shifted to happy mode.

Finn grabbed a napkin from the small piles Jessica placed everywhere and took another nibble. Setting them on an empty bookshelf, she dragged a stool over and started shelving from the nearest box. Landing here was hard enough without a bunch of books she wanted nothing to do with. She would arrange them nicely, at least.

Brushing her fingers over some of the covers took her back to when she'd read them and imagined she was the heroine and Brandon was her hero. She wasn't sure how she could have gotten him so wrong and thought they were compatible, but it concerned her. She didn't understand men, clearly.

The little bell over the door tinkled, signaling someone had entered the entry area separated off from the main room, with its framed quotes. Whoever it was might need an industrial pocketknife to hack through the jungle of plants brought from her big-city store. Sometimes she teased that only she and Jessica knew how to navigate past them.

A man in a cowboy hat strode in, not slowed down by a few spider plants and an overachieving philodendron or four. Something about his broad chest under his plaid work shirt with a fit that showed muscles on muscles drew her attention. His jeans were slung low on his slim hips, and she couldn't look away from him as he went up to the counter. Finn swallowed.

"Nice to see you, Clint." Jessica knew him, so she could easily get introduced. Not that she wanted to meet him.

She forced herself to go back to shelving books and straightened one she'd put in upside down. *Focus, girl.*

Oh wait, the name Clint rang a bell. She nearly laughed out loud at her pun, since he had made the overhead door jingle as he entered. When she'd sat in on a town meeting months ago, Jessica'd shown her the ropes. She didn't remember the guy at the meeting looking like *that* though. He'd been seated, partially hidden by the crowd, and now his height and the way he carried his lean frame screamed confidence, with a smile that hinted at his playful side.

What had gotten in to her? Her time was maxed out with getting her business going and helping Jessica. If she'd been interested in a man, it would be someone in a suit and Italian loafers, like those who poured out of the office building by her old place. Like her ex once had, actually.

She sneaked another peek. The cowboy hat was kinda cute,

though, and went with the stubble on his strong jaw line. Maybe God had plans for her she wasn't aware of.

Or maybe this uneven floor would swallow her up to save her from herself.

He lifted his hat, and ran his long fingers through his thick, dark sandy-shaded hair before replacing it. Jessica handed him a cup of coffee.

He took the cup and flashed a smile with teeth white enough to melt her socks off like some cowboy book cover models. "You've twisted my arm. Add a cinnamon roll. Can't resist 'em."

He turned and looked directly at Finn, catching her off guard, and she realized she'd been staring. Heat rose in her cheeks as their gazes locked. Even from this distance, his eyes radiated the deep shade of blue from her favorite beach read's book cover. Her stomach did a little flip.

Jessica came back with the cinnamon roll. "Here you go!"

He turned back for his food and to pay.

Jessica gave the slightest hand motion, hidden from the cowboy's view behind the counter, for Finn to come near, like Jessica seemed to sense she wanted to.

She gave a short shake of her head conveying not to bring her into the conversation. No point in meeting him when she didn't have the time or bandwidth to get to know anyone.

Jessica let out a low whistle, something she'd lately been taught as a way to relax. She used it to get Finn's attention when they weren't working close by.

Finn planted her feet in front of the stool just as Clint glanced her way again.

"Finn, you remember Clint Galloway from the town meeting on solar panels?"

She didn't know he was one of the Galloways, a family of brothers who were wealthy with farmland. Even more reason to steer clear. They tended to be in the spotlight, where she didn't want to be.

He grinned. A spark of something like amusement or that

playfulness she'd detected came through, which appealed to her. "Aw, come on. I'm not a bad guy." He took a sip from his coffee. "Well, depends on who you ask."

Finn got up and went toward the bakery side, willing her cheeks not to turn even more pink, which had never worked her whole life. She plastered a smile on her face and coped how she always had—by channeling the heroine in a favorite book from when she was a teen.

When she came close, she responded. "Being good is so over-rated." That hit the right tone she wanted. It didn't pay to be unfriendly, especially when she was trying to launch a business in a small town. Business was her only motivation in this.

He leaned a little more in Finn's direction, his scent a combination of the outdoors, the cinnamon from the roll, and coffee. He looked toward one of the tables Jessica had set up in The Sweet Shop area. "Care to join me over on the dark side?"

"Thanks, but I prefer the bright side." It wasn't a great comeback. Why had she carried on this line of conversation? Words from any book that would be helpful in this situation failed her.

A bell jingled overhead and a man in uniform wearing a badge stepped in. The wind caught the door and held it open for a second. A medium-sized brown dog rushed in right behind him, then swirled around Finn's feet, pushing her off balance.

The motion propelled her toward Clint, and she scrambled to stay upright. He managed to wrap his muscular arm around her shoulder and pulled her toward him. His face with its steel-cut jaw registered the surprise she shared, and his firm mouth opened slightly. Up close like this, he had to be the most handsome man she'd ever seen.

Finn's breath caught in her throat as a tickle in her nose warned of her dog allergy. She turned her head just in time. "Achoo!" His warmth around her was heaven. Too shocked to move, and not really wanting to, she held her ground. Pushing him away would be rude, wouldn't it? She sneezed again.

The officer cleared his throat. "I'm Charles Parker, here on official business."

Jessica walked around their shop, using coaxing tones. "Nice doggie, you can't be in a food business."

Clint's deep voice rumbled as he stood beside Finn. "I'm pretty sure I know what this is about. You can tell Louella that she's not going to get custody of Lilly."

What? Clint had a child? Then he must have a wife somewhere. Not that any of this mattered. Finn needed to get out of his arms, though. But his grip was firm. Not violent, but she couldn't find the will to slip away. If she did, it would cause more commotion. The sheriff didn't seem impacted by Clint's response.

Clint didn't give up, though. He stood tense beside her, his muscles taut and not in a good way. "You need to let her know there're things that've changed with me. First of all, she's not right in the head or she wouldn't try to take a child from her father. She's wrong to think I'm not a good influence. That couldn't be further from the truth."

"I'm just here with the papers. Save it for the judge. Having a woman in a kid's life sure would be nice. It's a shame her mom died."

"Charlie, I'm just going to prove to you what I'm saying. Come over here. Meet Finn. Uh, she's my fiancée." Finn couldn't believe what she was hearing. She saw stars like she might faint. "She's the best thing that's happened to me and Lilly in a long time, ever really. Maybe if Louella hears about Finn, she'll back off."

It was a good thing the sheriff had shown up. Finn didn't know what she might do to this Clint guy.

Chapter Two

Clint Galloway glared at the sheriff invading his space at the bakery. "And another thing. Lilly's got five aunts at least. I've lost track of the women in her life, so don't go making assumptions." In shock he'd claimed Finn Moore as his fiancée, his heart raced. He wasn't handling this well. But the man had papers in his hands that could ruin Clint's life.

Finn's fruity scent wafted up and her curves pressed next to him might be the only things keeping him sane. He caught Finn's blue eyes that sparked with anger, possibly mixed with confusion.

She took the palm of her hand, shoved him in the chest, and put some distance between them. "Your... your... " She spluttered on a long pause, then spoke like somebody from an old movie or something. He wasn't sure. "Oh, Mr. Galloway, your creativity's what interested me most about you. You can't go saying things like this in front of a sheriff." Her drawl like a southerner from his native Tennessee surely meant she was teasing him.

The sheriff studied him. "Seems like we've been missin' each other. I tried to catch you at the mill yesterday and Delaney's the day before."

"Didn't know I had to print my schedule." He couldn't loosen his grip on the woman beside him. After everything he'd been through as a kid, normally, nothing fazed him—except when it came to his fourteen-month-old daughter, Lilly.

Finn had tensed beside him, but then her shoulders relaxed underneath his fingers. At least she wasn't going to call him out—for now. He released the breath he'd been holding.

From the corner of his eye, a skirmish was happening outside the window involving a teenager on the sidewalk talking with Jessica. They wrestled the dog onto a leash.

Clint fought to concentrate, as his thoughts ping ponged everywhere. Desperation could do that.

"Louella's been threatening me. But I didn't know you were looking for me." One fib led to another, just like people said. Yelling his frustration would've felt good. But it was an indulgence he couldn't afford. He didn't want to be hauled in for disturbing the peace or something. So he held up the bag with the roll instead. "A man has to fetch a roll, ya know? Here, have this. Jessica'll get you a coffee. It's on me."

The sheriff grunted. "I don't think so."

Clint might as well push the limit and really convince this guy. He managed to come close enough to brush his lips over Finn's forehead. Her skin was incredibly soft, and if he wasn't mistaken, her eyelids fluttered shut for a moment. So he wasn't the only one feeling something between them.

It was tough to miss her gorgeous, flaming red hair and the way she paid sharp attention to everything that went down at the hotly debated town meeting. If Cam, his twin, hadn't been making a scene just by the fact he was opposing Wyatt Galloway's solar company and they were all half-brothers, Clint would've figured out how to meet Finn that night.

The sheriff came toward them. "I'm done messin' around. Take these papers now, or I'm gonna have to haul you in." Charlie stepped closer with a thick pack of papers tucked under his elbow and shoved a document and a pen toward Clint. "Here, sign for these and I'll get outta your hair."

Clint stood back from Finn with his food order. "Would you mind holding these, Finny?"

Her eyes opened wide but she did as he asked. He accepted the papers, then wrote his name big and in one flourish like he was John Hancock signing the Declaration of Independence. He'd only been a Galloway a little over a year, since he and Cam, his twin, found out who their real dad was. Life could be strange. His life, anyway.

After handing the signed paper back, he reached into the envelope and his gaze dropped to the first page. The words, "petition for sole custody of Lilliana M. Galloway to Louella Fenstamaker," kicked him in the gut.

Over my dead body. He shot up a prayer. *Forgive me, Lord.* As hard as things had been when he was young, they'd worked out eventually. He had to trust they would again. He wouldn't lose his little girl, whatever it took.

"Ms. Fenstamaker's been after me to make sure to deliver the papers. Guess I've done my job. Sorry it's not good news."

His ex-mother-in-law shouldn't have gone through with this. He lifted his hat and ran his fingers through his hair. "Well, if you talk to her..."

"Oh, I'm sure I will. She's called me every day, more than once."

"Let her know I'm engaged, would you please?"

"Sure, whatever." Charlie shook his head. "They don't pay me enough." He turned his back on them to leave.

Finn moved away, her cheeks still flushed, and Clint registered how alone he really was. Weird as it sounded, having her in his arms had helped him. Too bad he'd blown his chance to meet her naturally and get to know her. An ache landed in his chest. So much for crushing on her on his previous run to the bakery. He'd glimpsed her leaving out the back exit. Her rounded figure with that red hair and the strength in how she walked had mesmerized him.

The door jingled as the sheriff went out, and the sound

cleared his thoughts. A customer came in and Finn spoke to her. Clint grabbed his phone from his shirt pocket, checked the time, and then made a beeline toward the exit.

Since the customer had moved over to the books on her own, he spoke to Finn. "I've got an appointment I really can't be late for. Thanks so much and I'm sorry. I'll be back to explain... and to ask a favor I don't have the right to ask."

From the door, he thought the edges of her mouth might have turned up, except her eyes weren't really smiling. "You weren't kidding about the dark side. Hey, you forgetting something?" She held up his food and drink order.

"Like I said, I'll be back."

"Like that actor in the Exterminator, huh?"

"Exactly." His words floated over to her as the door was closing, leaving him on the sidewalk. Through the window, she gave him a tiny wave. Or maybe she was just corralling that mass of hair. He wouldn't be forgetting *her* anytime soon.

Clint sprinted down the street toward his truck he'd parked in front of Hit the Nail hardware, then hauled himself inside the cab on the seat. The papers filled up the glove box and he latched it closed before driving off. By pushing the speed limit, he pulled into the lane that led to Galloway Sons Farm in the nick of time, tapped on the second largest farmhouse's door and heard a voice.

"Come in." It had to be Annie, one of his sisters-in-law. His youngest half-brother Caleb's wife was watching Lilly for him.

He started for the knob and the door swung open with Max standing there, holding Lilly. His half-brother Wyatt's son wasn't quite four years old. But he carried Lilly in front of him with steady, sturdy fingers. His smile beamed at her, with his front baby tooth akilter like it might be getting loose. "Lilly, your daddy's here."

Clint's heart melted. When he had accepted Lilly needed to be with her mother, his ex-wife, that meant she lived across the country. But then Trixie's death in a car accident had put his daughter into his daily life. He was sorry for her loss. But he appreciated being with his daughter every day. Now Louella Fenstamaker had unleashed her grief, mental challenges, and vindictive nature to try to take Lilly from him.

"Boo." Max had a special connection with Lilly.

She let out a cute, shrill shriek and buried her face in Max's shoulder.

The sound made Clint shake his head to refocus. "You're like her big brother, more than a cousin. Lilly-Bear, how was your morning?"

Taking her in his arms, Clint inhaled her little girl scent of lotion and fruit, filled with awe he knew her everyday routines so well.

The smile and the glow in her innocent eyes said it all. "Daddy, I pet doggie."

"Wow! Did Annie feed you applesauce, sweet girl?"

She nodded up and down a few times. "App sos."

Annie appeared at the door with her baby on her hip. The Galloways were all about children, watching them for each other, too. They did it to help-out and to keep the little cousins close. He was totally in for it, with his Lilly loving every minute.

Annie kissed her baby's head. "I'm sorry you needed to get Lilly early. But Suzy-Q here's ready for her check-up."

"Thanks for fitting us in at all."

"You're family. Don't think a thing of it." Those were the sweetest words, and he didn't take them for granted, not ever.

He went into her living room, which was strewn with papers everywhere, on every surface. Annie had a heart of gold and if there was anything she and Caleb struggled with, it was how she kept house. She shoved some baby clothes over on the sofa for him to sit down. They chatted as he collected his girl's things and placed them in their designated spots.

She jiggled Suzy in her arms and watched him. "Wish I was that organized. How've you been?"

He dodged eye contact. "Can't complain."

He tucked Lily into her car seat, then carried her in it, along with everything else, to his truck. The pressure in his chest didn't let up. He kept it together and didn't spill the marbles to Annie that his world might fall apart, saying nothing about the papers.

He left them and went over to his truck and put Lilly in her car seat facing backwards. He kissed her heart-shaped face, her long lashes already almost resting on her cheeks.

He waved to Max and Annie and started the short drove to where he lived with Cam on the outskirts of the huge acreage of Galloway farmland. Lilly fell asleep right away. Driving along a gravel side road, he passed fields that filled him with praise to God for where he'd landed. He might have doubted Him during some very rough years but not anymore.

They'd learned their father was John Galloway, and he'd known Mom, a couple nights before his discharge from the U.S. Army in Tennessee. John had left for home in Indiana not knowing Mom was pregnant. Dad had fallen in love with his hometown sweetheart and their mother had died young, never able to tell them who their father was.

Clint pulled his truck up to the barn that had been renovated into a nice home with big wooden beams in the ceilings. Their newfound family had generously offered it to them. He shut off the vehicle and got out of the car to get Lilly.

"What's wrong?" Cam stood on the porch, a total surprise. Except sometimes they had a second sense about what was going on with each other.

"Nothin,' Camry." He liked using nicknames.

Clint busied himself unlatching Lilly's car seat, careful not to wake her. The papers were safe, for now. He pulled away from the back seat with Lilly and shut his truck door.

"Come on. You look like you've seen a ghost. Now, we can do this the hard way or the easy way."

Clint walked toward the barn that was home. "That's a tough call. You know I enjoy pain."

All his life, Cam had been able to pry information out of him. He was older, by a few minutes, but it seemed to have made all the difference. Sometimes Clint held out for weeks, like the time they'd both been interested in dating the same girl at school. Nothing this serious, though.

They entered the house, and he busied himself unpacking Lilly, but not in any hurry. All the while Cam stayed by his side. Lilly's eyes fluttered open, wide awake. He played a gentle game of peek a boo with her blanket covering her face and taking it away in surprise. Then he freed her from the blanket. Went to the refrigerator and put in the last of her apple sauce Annie'd sent. Anything to avoid eye contact with his twin.

He shut the refrigerator door. "I was served papers today."

Cam frowned. "What haven't you told me? You know that's against the twin code."

Clint gazed overhead to what had once been the haymow. It had been transformed into a loft with a huge bedroom and luxurious living space, too. Oh, how he'd like to go there and pretend this wasn't real.

"Louella's made rumblings about custody of Lilly. Her mom and I barely managed with the woman while Trixie was alive. After she died, once I really got settled in, just me and Lilly-Bear, we planned a grandma visit, told Louella as much. But she'd been impatient. One thing we'd agreed on was my having sole custody."

Or he thought they had.

Cam ran his fingers through his hair in the way Clint did in these situations. Having a mirror image of himself was a comfort at times. Like now, when he might lose the life he'd worked so hard to build.

"You're her father, a good dad by every reasonable standard. No court will take her from you."

"Some people won't listen to reason, like Louella. What rock have you been under? Courts'll do about anything."

He lifted Lilly from her car seat and didn't need to sniff to know she needed a change. Slinging her diaper bag over his shoulder, he snuggled her to his chest and directed his steps toward the upstairs to their loft.

"The family has lawyers on retainer. Don't make yourself crazy over this."

His foot landed on the first step and he marched on up. "On the chance it'd help, I let it slip to the sheriff that I'm engaged."

Cam's long, loud groan followed him up the stairs and lingered near the ceiling.

Once in her room, Clint plucked out a teething ring he kept in a basket of toys by the changing table. Lilly grabbed it as he laid her down. He fell into a rhythm with changing her diaper. There was a soothing sensation in doing something well, in caring for someone other than himself.

Her top had applesauce on it, and drool because the poor kid was teething, so he chose a new one for her.

Louella probably had news stories about him that painted him out to be a playboy. He'd been working in his thriving photography business before becoming a Galloway and coming to the farm. Many beautiful women were around him, in highly public places. Once there'd been a report of drugs at a party, and Louella'd likely run with something like that.

It was false. He'd never done drugs. He and his ex had been separated at the time. That didn't make him untrustworthy. He might have handled things better. When you grew up in foster care like he and Cam, since Mom died young... there was baggage surrounding feeling accepted. He'd liked the attention his clients gave him, and who d didn't enjoy being around pretty women?

Lilly was freshened up and he decided to put on a new shirt, then checked himself out in the mirror. The new pair of jeans and cowboy boots in his closet would be an important upgrade, not that he wanted to impress Finn or anything.

Seeing Finn again, maybe he could make a new first impression. It felt too soon after being thrown into his nightmare, yet he'd told her he'd come back.

In minutes, he went downstairs. "Would you please take care of Lilly while I run an errand?"

Cam pinned him with his gaze. "We'll go with you."

"Trust me. There's no need for that." If Cam was along, he might see he was interested in Finn for more than his fake fiancée.

"I want to hear more about your fiancée. Can't have you buying a farm or something." He made quotes with his fingers, "On the chance it'd help."

What was the big deal? It wasn't like he was prone to making rash decisions. He could afford anything he wanted anyway. The photography business had been very good to him. And his next venture at the farm, when he began a service breeding horses, would add to his wealth.

Clint put his face close to Lilly's and when she scrunched up her button nose, he rubbed noses with her. She giggled. "Ek, ek."

"Good!" She remembered him reading her the little Eskimo book and rubbing noses.

He refocused on Cam. "I'll be stopping off at Wind in the Willows, the book shop. I left something with Finn Moore, and I don't want Lilly to be there." She wouldn't understand their conversation. But he didn't want her near, just in case. Plus, he didn't know how it would go with Finn, now that she'd been thinking about what happened for hours.

"I'll ask Sierra to watch Lilly and come with you."

"No. That'd be strange." The knot in his stomach tightened. It was going to be strange anyway.

"She won't mind. It's her day off running Delaney's."

His brother wouldn't budge but Clint fought him anyway. He found Lilly's sun hat on the table and placed it on her head. She whipped it off in a second, her curls flying. "Camry, I don't need you to babysit me."

Cam caught the hat on his finger as it whizzed by. "I'll stay in the bakery. You won't know I'm there. I've wanted to stop in, see Jessica."

His brother's ulterior motive almost made it okay. He'd pretend to babysit Cam, who tended to be shy and unlucky at love.

Cam picked up his cell phone and headed out the door as he

connected with Sierra, warning her they would drop off Lilly. Clint tied Lilly's hat on and followed him out.

They got to the big house, and she shrieked to see Max again. He'd just come home. She didn't notice when her daddy left.

He knew Cam wouldn't tell him anything more and Clint wasn't going to share either.

But after dropping off Lilly, Cam said, "Since we're free, let's go check on the horses and make a list of what we need for spring before we head out."

Sounded good to him. Having to explain to a red-haired beauty why he'd made a pretend engagement proposal—and get her to keep it—had him dragging his feet.

What wouldn't go wrong with that idea? For a guy who had inherited five half-brothers in the past year, all of them married with kids, potentially just about everything.

Those legal papers in his glovebox proved it. Maybe they'd better stop off at the florist on the way, to improve his luck.

Chapter Three

Finn poked a pale pink, yellow, and blue swirled cardboard sign into a wire holder so it stood up. Carrying it over to the vintage electric fireplace on one wall of Wind in the Willows, she checked the wording: Submit essays for the Easter anthology here! A big basket on the mantel was perfect for her to place the sign behind, and a place to collect people's entries.

The Fair Creek Community Easter Egg hunt was one of the most popular events of the year, Jessica claimed. She didn't know what she'd do without her own personal town grapevine, not that they agreed on everything.

Finn had wanted to get involved with the hunt. She'd put a call out asking for essays with an Easter theme. She was still in the process of turning it into some kind of fundraiser for next year's hunt. It was a way for her to show people the advantages of having a town bookstore. She'd only gotten a few essays from people so far, but she was hopeful.

"Maybe he's not coming back." Jessica came up and stood beside her elbow.

Finn put the pages of her own essay, fastened together with a paperclip, into the basket. "Who?"

Jessica rolled her eyes. "That cinnamon roll won't be very

fresh in that waxy bag if Clint doesn't get here soon. Maybe I should transfer it to an air-tight one. His mug of coffee went down the drain hours ago."

Finn's thoughts had been a jumble of questions since he'd left and now it was nearly three o'clock. But she wouldn't give Jessica the satisfaction. She'd never get in a messy situation like this. "What difference does it make? I'm sure it was a temporary need, and he's moved on. He's forgotten all about us."

That was for the best, too.

"If it'd been me, I'd have shown Clint the door if he tried to pull that stunt."

Finn went over to an antique, dark wood table off to the side. Days ago, she'd chucked her small, white decorative tree made of rope-covered wire onto it. "Guess I'm not you." As she spread out each limb, she switched topics. "I really hope we get some more essays. I'll make a nice-sized booklet to hand out."

Jessica followed her over and began hanging the tiny ornaments of painted cows, eggs, and chicks carved out of wood. "Maybe your essay idea will work out." Finn plugged the little string of lights she'd picked up at the dollar store into an extension cord on the floor. They twinkled on and outlined the tabletop perfectly, beaming brightly to put a glow in the room.

Her morning events seemed to have given her a burst of energy. "Gotta admit, being in on a little drama was the most excitement I've had in a while. Pathetic, I know." Now that it was over, she could see the humor in the situation. It had jolted her out of her low energy mode, anyway.

"Nothing about you could ever be pathetic. I don't like it when you talk that way. You handled it well for your personality, I'd say."

Jessica always called her a people pleaser but today, it didn't bother her. Some things might be worth agreeing to.

The bell over the door jingled. Butterfly wings fluttered in Finn's stomach.

Clint was gorgeous, like he'd gotten more handsome since this morning. His shirt looked new, and his jeans didn't show any wear. His smile almost sparkled. "Brought you something."

In his large hand, he held out a sunshine-yellow ceramic pot. It had a smiley face painted on and a small philodendron peeked out.

"Plants are my love language."

A smile spread across his face. "Didn't want you to run low on plants. Not gonna be happy till I need a machete to whack my way in here." He laughed and his cowboy hat was set back far enough on his head that he slammed it down to keep it from falling off.

She smiled, and then joined him in laughing, which relaxed her tense muscles.

His entry had taken all her bandwidth and now she noticed his brother behind him, obviously his twin. Jessica introduced her to Cam and then they moved into the bakery part, leaving Finn and Clint to themselves.

Expectation crackled in the air as Finn took the potted plant, electricity shooting up her elbow when their fingers touched. "There's a high shelf this will be perfect for."

"Want me to help you put it there?"

An appreciation for his size, and how he made her feel small despite her curves, washed over her. Finn nodded. "Saves me from getting out the ladder." They went together and he placed it right where she would've chosen. "Thanks so much. You didn't have to. But getting me a plant's the way to my heart."

He quirked an eyebrow. "Consider it an engagement gift. The ring's coming."

She wrinkled her forehead in concern. "What? You've skipped the important part. Popping the question."

He might as well have wiped the smile off his face, it disappeared so fast. "Like I told Charlie, my ex-mother-in-law's planning to paint me as irresponsible. She's trying to take custody of my baby. I had to do something showing commitment. I still do."

Finn's heart rate kicked up and she reached for the stool she kept hidden away under plant vines for when she watered. Once seated on it, she found her strength for the conversation. "Wish you could find another way to pull off this scheme. You had no right to involve me." Her tone was sharper than she intended.

He took off his hat and ran his fingers through his hair. More like pulled his hair, seeming somewhat distraught. "I wish I hadn't. I really do. Something came over me and I'm sorry. I was desperate."

She wanted to stroke his hair.

What was happening to her? As she thought of the circumstances, which were all she could think about, a small part of her was relieved. At least he wasn't a criminal like she'd thought he might be at first. Maybe playing along hadn't been the worst thing, for such an important reason.

She reached for her watering can, stood up and began letting drips go into the pots. It was soothing and her heartbeat settled. "I *might* consider it. If you named me somewhere on the record, and I wouldn't have to do anything?"

What was she even thinking? She'd never been in trouble with the law and wasn't going to start now. Truth was everything.

He stood behind her and watched the water dripping onto the dirt. "I wish. She's the type to get a private investigator and follow me around. There's nothing she won't do to get her way. If you met Lilly, you'd understand my need to protect her."

His woodsy, soapy sent wafted up and she inhaled. Water started overflowing from a spider plant's pot and she put the can down. "You can't possibly mean to involve your child in this, to have me meet her. Not that I know anything about kids."

"I've thought about that. Lilly's not even two. Kids have sitters all the time that they get close to. It'd be like that."

The weather had kicked up into a warm day, and the entry way was in the beating sun. She felt perspiration drip down her back. All she knew was the tragedy of being taken advantage of, then having to give a baby up for adoption as a teenager. In some weird way, would this be a form of redemption, helping this man keep his baby?

She didn't even want children, not anymore. When she'd left Brandon, it had broken her heart. She'd put everything she'd thought she wanted out of her mind. Through prayer, God had shown her the way, how to be single.

Or so she'd thought. What would it be like if this situation was real and someone wanted to create a life together with her?

She moved to her favorite philodendron, Herbie. Clint waited for her answer, not saying anything. They wouldn't win at this game of secrets. "I don't see how we can pull it off. Will anyone believe us?"

"Yes, they will." He looked directly into her eyes. "Anybody can see how a guy could fall madly in love with you. Will you help me, help us, Lilly and me?

Her heart thumped in her chest, and she couldn't help letting a smile show. Her wounded spirit wanted to believe, if only for a moment, that a man was capable of loving her the way she wanted to be loved. Deserved to be loved.

No way that could be Clint Galloway. In this small room, surrounded by plants, a girl could drown in those blue eyes of his, though.

Lord, help her.

"Look, we'll make it as much fun as we can. Our family and friends love us. I mean, my family adores me. Hahaha. They'll understand when we tell them the truth, after the judge awards me full custody. This really should go my way. I'm just looking for an insurance policy more than anything. What do ya' say, Finny?"

"I'll find some insurance companies for you to call?"

He laughed and it was light and airy. She laughed, too and it had some part of nerves to it.

"Look, my brother and I were foster kids. I'll do everything in my power for Lilly to stay with me."

She swallowed. "You got me there. I gave up my baby when I was in high school. Somebody took Emily in, and I pray every day they were a wonderful family for her." Her eyes filled with tears, and she blinked them away, almost. "I don't like we'll be deceiving everyone."

She couldn't believe she was going to go through with this. That stubble on his chin was killer, and she wondered if she'd get her heart broken all over again.

His handsome mouth and perfect nose came closer, and her pulse kicked up.

Would they have to kiss to convince people? A shiver went up her spine.

So what if they did? If somebody had to smooch with Clint Galloway, she'd be the bigger person and make the sacrifice.

She needed to get herself back on track. "If we're doing this, we're going to have to learn more about each other, practically have relationship 101 classes. And I'll want a big, fat breakup. I couldn't handle a confession that we lied. Quick, what's your favorite color?"

"It's green. Look, I can't ask you to do this kind of favor for nothing. And you're being such a good sport about it. My family's helped others with their tornado damage. Community service is important to us. In return for supporting me to keep Lilly, I'll help fix this place up."

He'd flipped the scales. It'd take the pressure off her book sales. Maybe she'd even save face with her best friend and not seem foolish. "Jessica owns the building, and that'd be great, for both of us. Oh, and maybe we set some ground rules? No saying 'the l-word'—love for the crowd, okay?"

Why did she feel she might need that guideline? Because falling hard was her go-to move, if her history was anything to go by.

"Are flowers and plants off-limits, too then? What about writings and singing outside someone's window?"

"I wouldn't want to squelch anyone's creativity. Nope, not me. Croon away. My window's on the second floor right here where we're standing."

He reached for her hand. "It's a deal then. Maybe this'll be training to improve my luck with the opposite sex."

"Don't get your hopes up. I'm not exactly a success with that either. You better not take tips from me." They were half-way to a handshake when the outer door opened. Both of them startled. Disappointment at missing out on his touch nudged its way in Finn's brain.

She might be in trouble here.

Ted and Elizabeth stepped in, and couldn't have looked more unsurprised, even pleased, to see them huddled there.

Everybody said the woman's face looked ten years younger since she'd married Ted. She glowed. "I'm so glad we caught you two together! We just heard the news and wanted to congratulate you both!"

Elizabeth put her arms around her, and Finn leaned into the strength of the hug.

Clint blinked like a raccoon that'd been asleep in a dark shed. Finn knew she had to have that same expression. Neither said a word.

Elizabeth dropped her arms and looked at Ted. He shrugged, a man comfortable with being clueless with women, she decided.

Finn finally found her voice. "How did you find out?" She chirped, her voice a little off, but at least she hadn't confessed to being engaged.

Elizabeth patted her dark hair with some salt and pepper. A crease appeared on her forehead and her eyes held alarm. "Why? Is it supposed to be a secret? Are we wrong about this?"

Ted's eyes shone and he put his pointer finger to his lips, then removed it. "We'll never tell. But once news hits Delaney's, it's like a vortex and there's no putting it back in the bag."

Anyone could have spilled the news. They'd been standing in the middle of the bakery this morning when the sheriff showed up. Clint still hadn't said anything.

It hit Finn like a ton of books falling from a shelf. He was leaving it up to her. Here was her chance to stop the rumor mill and correct things. Taking down the engagement chat, like sticking a pin in a balloon, could start right here, with her.

But she didn't want to. What if Lilly really *did* need her to pretend to be engaged to her dad? If there was a chance, she had to do it. Clint must have a reason to be concerned. Was there something he wasn't telling her?

She beamed her best look of adoration toward Clint and pretended to straighten his collar, like he was all hers. "It's just, uh, we haven't known each other *that* long. You know what they say, life comes at you fast."

Clint reached over, put his arm around her shoulder, and shook Ted's hand with the other. "We're still getting used to it ourselves. Things happened so quickly."

An understatement, if there ever was one.

Elizabeth gave Finn a side hug. "Welcome to the family." She'd forgotten the woman was an aunt in the Galloway clan. "People are thrilled for you! We didn't take very long either, did we honey? Ted, dear!" He was talking March Madness with Clint, and Finn knew only that it was basketball. Elizabeth went on. "When you know, you know, like the kids say."

Finn nodded. Sports weren't her thing. She needed to learn a whole lot more about this man she was engaged to. What if they had nothing in common and everybody saw through them?

Chapter Four

Clint waited while Finn tended her plants some more. Her fingers gently touched leaves and pressed the dirt, checking like they did on the farm. She made it look almost like a form of meditation, even calling one Herbie. He wondered how she'd be with Lilly.

This was all pretend, though.

It'd been a big day. He looked out the window of her business and glimpsed his aunt and Ted as they walked down the street after Finn confirmed their news. Ted guided his wife by the elbow when they came to a high curb, and again when they climbed into their golf cart. They seemed comfortable and seemed to enjoy one another. It would be nice if he felt that way about someone.

An image of his daughter's face popped into his head. Lilly deserved him to be the best dad he could, and he'd already spent time away from her on this engagement idea he'd hatched up. If it worked, it'd be worth it.

Reality check. He and Trixie had never been good together, not really. Maybe if he'd had an example growing up, things would have been different. He'd have known they weren't compatible. But switching around households and being with struggling families had been his only experience. Thankfully, social services managed to keep him and Cam together.

Lilly'd been the best part of his marriage.

Finn finished her fiddling and stood with some dead leaves in her hand.

Something about her warmed his heart, taking care of plants and books. They were his two favorite things. "Hey, thanks for backing me up. I'll never be able to thank you enough. Let's go tell the others. I'm a little hesitant. Cam's not only my best friend but my toughest critic."

She put her hand on his arm, and the warmth went through his sleeve, something he could get used to. "Jessica and I can be like that, too. I think we know each other so well and care so much, sometimes we get in our own way."

"We may as well start with those two now then, get our story together." He held out his hand and she placed hers in his as he pushed open the light-weight door.

Once in the main part of the business, he looked everywhere and only saw Jessica wiping out a food case, humming to some music coming through a sound system. "Where's my brother? What've you done with Cam?"

He didn't even know if humor was okay in this crowd.

Finn put her hands over her mouth in fake horror. "Maybe a monster kidnapped him. Or he was entangled in the plants and we never noticed?"

Clint laughed, and it felt good. Things were going to be okay. He dared to hope they might even be better than that. The big Galloway clan had changed his life and been a great addition he counted his blessings for, so he knew having more relationships, even a fake one, could bring more joy than he could imagine. He prayed it would be true.

Jessica continued her scrubbing, not even popping her head up to look at them. "He's been gone for a while, just grabbed a coffee and ran, basically. Since you two appeared to be in intense negotiations, I helped him sneak out the back door into the alley."

Finn's attention had been drawn to the bookstore side. Something made her face light up and had her heading to the little fireplace. "Do you think he's okay? Actually, lots of people use our back door to come and go."

"Pretty normal behavior for him, always doing his own thing." He pushed back his irritation. He'd wanted to get this over with, telling the two people they knew best, Jessica and Cam, about their plans at the same time. He couldn't shield Cam from his behavior. A little rough around the edges, the right woman would bring him around. Clint wondered if he'd want something more with Finn, in a genuine way, except relationships could be so unpredictable and never lasted. At least, his hadn't. But if he ended up with a friend, it wouldn't be all bad.

Jessica closed the display case and tossed the cloth in a sink behind her. "Good to know. He left really quickly, for no reason, if you ask me."

Finn came back to him, her hand full of papers. He inhaled in a deep breath, maybe because it was the second time today he'd been confronted with a stack of papers. Her smile was too wide for this to be bad news, though. "Look," she said, breathlessly. "These are essays people turned in for the anthology I'm planning. I've been posting it on social media, sending them to the library if they want to print it out. I'm taking emails too, but forgot to check it."

She reached for her phone, and he touched her arm. "You have every right to be into your own things, of course. I barged in on you and I'm sorry. But first, can we tell Jessica like we planned? Then I wanna go find Cam."

Finn's face fell a little, the corners of her mouth turning down slightly. He regretted that and wanted her smile back. He had a lot to learn about putting others first, and not just Cam his twin or Lilly.

Finn turned to her friend. "You know this morning, when the sheriff came, and I let Clint tell him we're engaged? He's told me we need to do that a while longer, because he's in a child custody battle. I've decided to keep up that charade and need you to keep our secret."

Jessica's eyes grew wide. Her mouth opened like she wanted to say something, only she didn't. This might be a first.

Finn rushed on. "I know it's not right maybe, or something you'd do."

Jessica went over and put her arms around Finn. "You seem determined to do this but I wish we'd discussed it first. I'll support you every way I can, like I always have. It sounds like it could be painful and you're my main concern."

"I've taken everything into consideration and think I can handle it. With you beside me, it'll be a whole lot easier."

"Whenever you decide to tell people the truth. That's going to be the hard part, you know, right?"

Clint had scaled these issues with Finn and was done. "I have some good news. For the time she's in the family, and because we're community-minded, we'd like to help fix up your building."

Jessica blinked, and blinked again. "What?! I've been so worried and the estimates are out of my budget. You'd really do that?"

"I'm a person of my word. I've not gotten off on the best foot, with any of this. But yes."

"I can't repay you. You understand that, right?"

"I don't expect anything from you in return. We probably shoulda offered before. You're not the only ones we will have helped. However you want to look at it, by keeping my secret, you're giving me the best chance at keeping Lilly, and that's more than enough repayment."

The woman's smile beamed so bright it filled the room. She did some kind of a two-step and nearly skipped over to Finn. "Put that phone down and hug me. Congrats on your engagement!" She did a little exclamation of excitement that sounded genuine to him.

Finn's face wasn't a match, since her smile didn't reach her eyes and her forehead had frown lines. "Thanks for taking this so well, better than I hoped."

"I can't wait to see this place looking good, the way it ought to. See, I can take other people's ideas." Jessica's smile was triumphant like she'd proved something. He wasn't sure what that was about, but she didn't wait for validation. "Especially when they make my dreams come true. And I think that little girl's pretty lucky to have a dad who cares that much. Mine never did."

"Everybody deserves good parents. I'm sorry that didn't happen for you." He felt bad for the woman, even though they'd just met. But she seemed to get what his custody crisis was really about. Although her saying her dad wasn't there for her made him sad, it also spurred him on to keep going.

He turned to his pretend fiancee. "Tomorrow night we're having a birthday party for Kayla's twins. She's the only sister in our bunch, my half sister, technically. I'm hoping you can come, to bring my family in on this. What do you say?"

She took a deep inhale. "Sounds great!" Her brightness didn't ring totally true, as if maybe she was putting her doubts aside.

"Okay, I'll text you the details. I can't wait for you to meet Lilly."

Finn held up her phone. "They may be the best pick-up line to get my phone number yet. Tell me and I'll type it in."

After he did, the two women started talking about the essays people had mailed in and he headed out. Jessica walked over to the wall that looked like it might bury them in rubble any minute. The construction couldn't start soon enough.

Now if he could only get Cam's blessing. But nothing ahead looked as difficult when compared to creating an engagement out of thin air.

And proving to a judge that relationship was real.

Chapter Five

Finn posed in front of the mirror in her bedroom. She'd bought the earrings on a whim and never worn them. The feathery things nearly swished down to her shoulders.

"Nope, looks like you're trying too hard." Jessica popped another Cheeto into her mouth. She rearranged herself cross legged on a vintage upholstered side chair that'd been in the apartment when she'd inherited the building. Its floral pattern screamed the 70s.

Finn lifted her arms to show how the shacket flowed. "But I've always thought this teal shade brings out the color of my eyes."

"You're not wrong. But that style of fringe went out in the 90s. It's not comin' back in our lifetimes. Trust me. Fashion fades for a reason."

Feeling feisty, Finn undid the buttons, tossed it on the heap of discards on her bed, and grabbed for the snack bag. "Surely you know everything comes back around eventually? Think elephant bellbottoms. Hey, give me some."

"Not until you're done with the clothes, don't want everything dusted in orange. Next, try that spaghetti strap romper."

"I'll freeze." She put it on anyway. "You're probably the only from-scratch baker that eats junk food."

"Nope, when we go to conferences, the munchies are the main attraction." Finn spun around in front of the mirror. "Now, I've got a shawl thing you could pull over it. But maybe it's not trying hard enough. Not time to pull out the sandals yet either."

They kept going, with Jessica dissing every outfit change, until time ran out and she had to leave. She climbed into her Pontiac Grand Prix she'd had since her twenties, her nerves grateful for the comfortable, soft denim shirt with a western vibe and some strategic frayed edges.

"You look great!" Jessica had come downstairs from the apartment to see her pull away from their gravel parking space out back of Wind in the Willows. "Remember, don't drink the punch. It might be spiked."

It was their holdover phrase from school prom.

"And another thing, remember my phrase about being honest with yourself? Nobody goes through trying on that many outfits for somebody they have no interest in."

Finn opted to let her friend have the last word. She waved before Jessica was too far to see. Having someone who knew her history felt like a gift from God most days, but being reminded of prom wasn't something she welcomed. Emily wasn't far from her mind, and just knowing Jessica knew that helped. Running from her past, and hiding details from Brandon, hadn't worked anyway.

She'd gone junior year with a guy she'd been fixed up with, like everybody did then. When he'd forced himself on her, she'd ended up pregnant. Jessica'd arranged for her to stay with her grandma, and she'd been back by second semester senior year.

The Galloway Sons Farm main house appeared out of nowhere. She'd been too lost in memories to pay attention on the drive. Clint had asked her to come a little before the festivities were starting.

She shut off the car and wiped her hands on her jeans. She'd never had nerves like these. Her car window was slightly cracked open from trying to get fresh air into her lungs. What was she doing?

"Hey, you're right on time." Clint came toward her from the other side of the house, with a little girl in his arms wearing a matching cowboy hat. A big old red barn was behind them could've been in a painting, and its side door stood cracked open. He was gorgeous and took her breath away. For a minute, she let herself think his wide smile was all for her, and for once she didn't let the baby remind her of what she'd missed, not too much, anyway. His perfectly aligned teeth and a slight bump on his nose she'd just noticed indicated it might have been broken at some point. Rugged had a better look than men in suits ever had. Who knew?

She took her time shutting off the car and tucked two little gift boxes into her purse before grabbing it and getting out. Deep breaths, Finn.

"Your instructions were pretty specific. Dusk is a time on the clock. I had no idea."

"This is Lilly. You missed the prettiest sunset a little while ago. Watching the sky's fun, right?"

The child could have starred in an ad for baby food. She plucked her hat off and her hair framed her face in waves. Standing together like that, the resemblance of their hair texture was striking. Their eye color was as deep as part of the sky over the fields. "Hi!"

"Hi, Lilly. Your dad's told me a little about you."

Lilly waved both her arms. "Hi!" Her little jean jacket and the tiny cowboy-look boots melted Finn's heart. This child was not only well loved but every detail was tended. Or maybe that was for the birthday party.

Finn patted her arm and smiled, at a loss for what to say. She had zero experience with children, and wanted to think it was due to circumstances. But now she questioned whether she had subconsciously been avoiding them.

Clint rescued her, whether he knew it or not. "I wanted to show you the baby chicks we have in the barn."

She walked beside them on the way. Thank goodness for Jessica's advice to wear ankle boots. They tramped over uneven lumps of roots sprinkled in among smooth patches and dormant grass waiting for spring. The ground could've been a map of her life. She had no idea what was coming next, or what the equivalent for ankle boots to face life might be. The essay she'd put in the anthology began to form in her mind.

Once inside the barn, Lilly let out a squeal. Clint set her down on the ground and she ran on sturdy legs to an area with the cutest little yellow chicks ever. The little girl went to the fencing around the chicks and made the little gate open to enter.

Clint went to a shelf and removed a camera with a longer lens than she'd ever seen, except on TV.

"Not a guy who takes photos on smart phones like the rest of us, huh?"

"Before I came here, I was a professional photographer. If you're impressed with this, you haven't seen anything yet."

It was a light-hearted remark but made her realize she didn't know anything about him. She probably couldn't play his fiancée on TV, not even if someone gave her a script.

He went over, knelt, and snapped pictures of his daughter. She bubbled over with oohs and ahhs as she picked up the chicks. Finn held her breath, wondering when she'd squeeze one too tight. Lilly seemed to know what to do, though. Once when she became agitated and seemed to be getting a bit hyper, Clint went to her and spoke softly to her, stroking her back.

When he returned to Finn, he held up his camera to show some of his shots.

"She's beautiful. You must be so proud of her. And your photography skills. All my shots are blurry or off-center."

He leaned near her ear. "Stick with me and you won't have to worry about taking pictures."

Finn's stomach did that little flutter thing. Something about the deepness of his voice and his closeness had to be the reason.

He clicked some more, and she remarked on her favorites. "Stop. That's perfect. What would you think about Lilly and the chicks on the cover of my Easter anthology?"

He put his hand over his heart. "Fine by me. She's photogenic, although I might be partial. I could put it in her scrapbook."

Lilly came out of the fencing and left the gate open. "You seem to really know all the great dad moves."

The chicks followed Lilly as she headed toward them. "I have my Galloway family to thank. It was pretty rough at first, for us both. Missing her mom, and she can't show it."

"She seems so, uh, perfect, I guess."

"Oh, she is. According to Annie, she's not saying as many words as she should. I'm supposed to read to her. My family's been the best thing for her, for me. When she came, I'd never really changed a diaper."

This was getting way too serious and she had nothing to add. "I feel like I ought to be taking notes or something. I'm listening, and care. But it reminds me of when the teacher said there'd be a pop quiz on the material."

Lilly marched around at their feet and the chicks swarmed around. "Here's the thing. We've told people it happened fast. You can just say you don't know something."

She took a deep breath and the tension in her chest eased. "I hadn't thought of that. People shouldn't be trying to trip us up anyway."

He swooped down and gathered Lilly in his arms. "Let's put the chickies back." She touched her hands on his scruff and Clint shook his head to tease her. She felt like she was intruding on a special moment.

Maybe he caught that feeling because he included her. "Hey, we need to be going. Could you put my camera back while I put them in? There's a case I zip it in to keep out dust."

She did as he asked and once the chicks were corralled, they returned.

They fell into step, with Lilly between them, and Finn held her hand. It was so little. Maybe Clint had the right idea about asking questions.

"I'd love to have you come to my story time at the bookstore."

"I'd like that. I keep up with what the doctor says, and she's not concerned, not yet anyway. I'm reading to her a lot, and so is Annie and anybody I can rope in. I'm hoping she'll grow out of it as she gets more comfortable."

Here was a subject she could warm up to. "I'm doing some special activities for Easter at Wind in the Willows. Lilly'll love it."

"That'd be great. Spending time with other children, especially if they don't complete her sentences for her, would be good."

They were almost to the door of the farmhouse. More cars were in the driveway. Her heart started to race. Was she ready for this? "I'm afraid we're late. I wanted to make a good first impression."

He moved Lilly to one side and slipped his arm around Finn's waist. "They'll wait. It's a pretty laid-back group. Lil-Bear, reach into daddy's pocket."

Finn took a deep breath, easing into his muscles and more than that, his support. He was easy to talk to. Maybe they'd become friends after all this.

Lilly pulled a tiny box out of her dad's pocket and put it in Clint's outstretched hand.

Then she stuck her fingers back in and brought out something small she popped into her mouth.

Finn gave him a questioning look and he answered before she could ask anything. "It's soybeans. They grow in the field, you know?"

"Do they now? There's a little book in my shop that explains the growing stages Lilly might enjoy."

Putting several soybeans in Lilly's tiny hand, he set her down on the back porch. With surprising grace for a man of his size, he managed to position himself on one knee before she knew what was happening. Finn gasped. Clint flipped open the box and pulled out a vintage ring with a medium-sized oval stone setting, one like she'd never seen before.

"Finny, will you be my fiancée?"

Unable to speak, she gave a nod, and he slipped the ring on her finger. Her heart was full, as silly as it seemed.

That twinkle in his eye she was getting to know well showed up again. "What we're doing may not be real. But there's nothing fake about my appreciating you."

"Okay now. I'm not crying. Or maybe I will, just a little."

Clint managed to rise and on his way to fully standing, he leaned in and brushed his lips over hers. She felt it down to her toes. Their connection was gentle and fleeting. She wanted more, in an urgent way that she hadn't wanted in a long time, if ever.

Flexing her fingers to make the ring more obvious, she showed him how it looked on her hand. "It's beautiful. Thank you. I'm feeling like I really am engaged."

"You're a sweetheart for doing this, for me and especially for Lilly. It's from our mother's things. Cam approves your having it."

Clint picked up Lilly and took Finn's hand. When he turned the doorknob and opened the door going into the family home, Cam scrambled away on the other side, like the door might smash into him.

He must have been standing really close. Had he been watching them? She touched her fingers to her lips, realizing she didn't care if he had.

She'd have to get used to people seeing them together.

Chapter Six

Finn stepped into the huge farmhouse with Clint by her side, carrying Lilly in his arms. The scent of his aftershave wafted up around them and she wondered if he'd taken extra care like she had. His black, Western-styled shirt made his eyes look dark, intense even.

Before she could process anything, a roar went up. "Congratulations!" came the nearly deafening shout, from a roomful of people, every one of them with smiles on their faces. Some men rushed over to Clint and slapped him on the back, while others pumped his hand in a vigorous handshake. A cluster of children, who could only be described as a pack, ran up to Lilly. They were screaming and jumping, and she joined right in. Her little jumps made Finn's heart swell.

A woman carrying a baby approached Finn. "I'm Annie. This is Suzy and she's three months old today. When Clint came to pick up Lilly this morning, I thought something was on his mind."

She didn't want to burst the woman's bubble and let her know Clint had been thinking about the sheriff's visit. Somehow, anything that might come out of her mouth seemed like it would be a false statement. She froze.

Annie's gaze dropped to Finn's ring finger, and Annie lifted her hand to see better. "Oh, that's gorgeous. I've never seen anything like it."

She smiled, and it wasn't faked. Here was something she could talk about safely. "It belonged to Clint and Cam's mother. As you can imagine, it means a lot to me. I feel special getting to wear it."

Annie released her hand and waved to someone. "Oh, come over here, Kayla."

A woman with dark hair pulled back into a ponytail, her many stray wisps a fringe around her face, waved back. She approached them and Annie introduced her.

"You've gotta meet the one sister in the Galloway sons."

That explained her striking features. "Welcome to the family! I hope you and Clint'll be happy together. He's a great guy, from the short time I've known him as my half-brother, anyway."

This was the kind of conversation she'd dreaded. Her fingers went to the ring on her finger and she spun it around and around. A new way to fidget, just when she needed it most. What should she say? Probably not, "You've known him longer than I have."

Kayla smoothed her hair and Finn was taken by the intensity in her dark brown eyes. "Don't mind me for saying that about Clint, noting he hasn't been my half-brother long. The party's for my twins and I'm distracted. Bye! Maybe we'll chat sometime."

"I'd like that. Clint thinks the world of you all."

Kayla nodded, as she swirled away.

She was drawn to how down-to-earth the woman was. It made her realize she'd been pretending for too long—way before Clint made her his fake fiancée. She'd tried to go on without facing how much giving up Emily had changed her life. Agreeing to a closed adoption had wrecked her.

Someone touched her elbow, like they were steadying her, and she looked up into Clint's eyes. She smiled, a genuine expression of emotion that she combined with sending him a message with her eyes: "Please rescue me from your family."

"Thanks again for watching Lilly for me today, Annie."

This conversation was common ground, safe territory even. When Annie shifted gears and described how well Max and Lilly got along, Finn let her gaze roam the room. The huge farm style kitchen had been turned into an Easter wonderland. There were white trees like hers in the shop, only these were life sized, and bunnies as big as people were standing under them. Glitter-covered eggs hung from their limbs. Huge wooden tables styled like picnic tables were set with paper plates with bunnies on them and a wood shelf at one end simply said "Easter" on it in bold letters.

She identified "Here Comes Peter Cottontail" playing in the background, now that the sound was down to a low roar. A rustic wooden cross filled the space in one corner, with a deep purple cloth draped around it.

"So, how'd you two meet?" Kayla had circled back just to ask that question. Being asked so directly reminded Finn of an inter-rogation, which stopped Finn cold in her tracks. A tension settled in her chest. They really did need to get their story straight.

As if on cue, Clint caught her eye and draped his arm over Finn's shoulder. "She can probably describe it best. But I'll give my version. By the way, Finn has a bookstore on Main Street in Fair Creek. It's called Wind in the Willows, and—

"Attention! Let's get this party started!" Abby, a friend of Jessica's, stood on a chair to get attention.

Finn let out a breath and whispered into Clint's ear, "Saved by the party."

After the loud voice, people kept talking, and someone clanked silverware on a glass until they stopped. "I'm Abby, Miles Galloway's fiancée, and mommy to our kids, Willow, Boone, and Dane. I'm the aunt to these twins. Today's their birthday. They're three! We've having an Easter theme!"

Two footstools had been dragged over near the kitchen island and a little girl and boy were lifted up, and each one stood on top of one. "Ella and Drew, wave to everybody! Let's sing 'Happy

Birthday.' Then we'll line up the kids and they'll march around playing their percussion instruments."

Finn might have thought the marching strange if she didn't know Abby owned a music store, The Melody Shop. If she hadn't seen this big family for herself, she might not have believed this existed anywhere other than magazines. The number of kids blew her mind. Everything was just so different from growing up an only child, without many relatives. She wondered if Emily, her baby, had siblings.

The singing and the kids marching with cymbals and little drums made it difficult to chat above the noise. But Finn smiled and breathed easier, waving at random people since she didn't have to wonder who would ask a question she couldn't answer. It was simply too loud to hear.

Clint led Finn over to the drink station and she grabbed a bottled water. She'd have plenty of sweets when it was time for dessert, given the two gigantic cakes. One was shaped like a bunny with a carrot and the other was a lamb with coconut for the fur. Little signs stuck in them indicated one was sprinkle cake and the other chocolate.

Clint leaned down close to her ear so she could hear over the noise. "I hope you're okay with all this."

"Your family's great. It's a little overwhelming and I'm sure I'd fail a quiz on naming them, especially the kids." She motioned for him to lean down and whispered. "No one said they're surprised about us."

He laughed. "True on both counts. My family's amazing, and even I might fail a quiz on them! Not really. But it's going to be hard for you when everyone's mingling together. Since we're all close, I appreciate not having to do much dad stuff once in a while, when they're around. They all help take care of Lilly when we're together. The guys and the women are all kid people."

"I can see why Lilly's getting along well here."

At least her words sounded good, hopefully. She'd never spent time around kids and accepted she would never would, since she'd booted Brandon. Her only child had been conceived under terrible circumstances. She couldn't check on her because it had been a closed adoption, and some days that really got to her.

Clint tossed an empty bottle for some kind of tea and lemonade combination into the recycle can. "This is all new for me. Bachelorhood was my intention after Trixie, my ex left—until Lilly needed me. That lifestyle I used to have that ended? Louella's using it against me."

"That seems so wrong. Even if you were wild before, and not saying that's true. But people can change. You've obviously been putting your daughter first."

She didn't believe *she* could change into a family person, though. This seemed like a lot of work, not something natural to her at all. Her peaceful life with books suited her. If only she could tamp down her angst, which showed up when she was running author events Jessica loved.

Drew zipped past wearing a banner that said "Birthday Boy" and a paper crown, waving a Star Wars lightsaber.

Clint looked around the room, shifting his weight from side to side. "Hey, this party's not for my age group. Why don't we go outside in the barn, and you can meet my brothers."

"That sounds like a plan." Maybe she'd stop being on edge if she didn't have to wonder when she'd meet the next Galloway family member. Seeing them together gave her half a chance of remembering them, too.

Clint headed out the door, stopping and letting a couple of people know where they were going, from what she could tell. When they got outside, he turned in a different direction from how they'd come in.

"One excuse is as good as any to spend time out in the barn. I think you'll like to see this."

A shiny metal barn at least triple the size of the one with chicks came into view. Going inside together, Clint walked over to three men, all with thick, dark hair. She could tell they were brothers. Each one sat on the cement slab floor on a bucket that had been turned over for a seat. Two of them had old metal canisters in front of them and were turning a crank to make ice cream the old-fashioned way.

A wave of nostalgia swept over Finn, remembering the only reunion her parents had taken her to when she was a girl. Great granddaddy had made ice cream. She longed to know what it would be like to spend so much time with family over so many years.

She ached for the old days and couldn't figure out what was hitting her so hard now.

Clint went over to the tallest brother who stood by an opened bag of ice. The man looked him in the eye and spoke firmly, except his eyes danced. "You can't have any. This is for the kids."

"Leo, you guys can't fool me that it's for the kids. You're hiding away so you can hear yourselves think."

The same brother had a comeback in seconds. "Hey, with our triplets entering the terrible twos, I'll go anywhere to get away."

There was a laugh and Leo raised his eyebrows, while others simply smiled. Finn wondered if Clint had gotten his sense of humor from the family genes, despite not growing up around them.

Clint took a wood rod propped on a wall by Leo. "It's fun and builds muscles to poke ice that hardens so much it doesn't move. But seriously, I wanted you to know Finn and I are engaged."

Each man's eyes seemed to widen, and Finn shifted her feet, waiting to hear their reaction. "Like he said, I'm Leo, the one with the triplets that'll duck into a closet if I can get more space. Guess we missed something hanging out in the barn after all. Congrats." The other two introduced themselves as Caleb and Wyatt, offering their congratulations.

Clint poked his stick up and down into the ice in the canister to break it up. "This builds muscle. We get to debate how much rock salt and ice makes the best Galloway secret recipe, too. But guys, I've offered to help Finn fix up the building with her bookstore and bakery and would like your help.”

She shuddered inwardly, not used to getting help, and certainly not asking for it. “Oh, please don’t feel like you have to, I’ll give you a minute to talk among yourselves.”

As she turned to give them space, Clint started toward her and she waved him off. Once she’d stepped away, the men talked and she assumed it was about her and Jessica’s place. Her gaze traveled around the barn, and she moved to get a better look at huge old tractor tires leaning on a wall, and buckets and a ladder randomly abandoned there. The dust was thick everywhere, partly from sawdust that drifted over from underneath an old saw mounted to a table.

The discussion ended and Clint came to her side, explaining they’d agreed to do the work, and she thanked them on her way out. The rest of the evening was a muddle with serving the cake and ice cream. She’d thought the birthday twins couldn’t get any cuter, but their little faces became like angels when they were covered in icing.

“Can Lilly spend the night?” Sierra had sneaked up behind them, with Lilly in her arms. The child’s eyes were droopy with a long time between blinks, and her head lolled on her aunt’s shoulder.

“She’d sleep better in her own bed.” Clint seemed like his mind was made up.

“If she stays, Lilly can sleep in a little tomorrow since Annie’s coming to get her kids later and will get her.”

Clint nodded and kissed his daughter good night. But he didn’t smile like he was happy.

When things were winding down, Clint walked Finn to her car. He took her hand to help her over the bumps. She hung on tight, for more reasons than navigating the physical bumps.

“Thank you for showing up tonight.”

“I wanted to.” She hadn’t exactly had a good time and needed to keep truth where she could.

They reached her car and after Finn popped the door locks, he opened her door. "This is a classic," he said. "Can we do lunch tomorrow, and maybe you can tell me about it and more."

She nodded and gave him a quick hug.

He pulled her back in. "Let's kiss. It's our engagement night."

Clint leaned in and their kiss she'd been unaware had been simmering underneath the surface broke through. Quick and yet deep, he had her heart racing, leaving her short of breath. Once they parted, reluctantly, she landed in her car seat weak-kneed.

He spoke into her ear. "I couldn't leave you without finishing what we started."

"You're going to make someone a great fiancé." She meant it and it left her a little sad.

She drove away and he gave a little wave as he got smaller in her rearview mirror.

Once she'd gotten herself home, Finn's energy left her. She dragged herself up the stairs and let herself in, glad she had her own entry and privacy. As an introvert accustomed to a small family, getting through the evening had taken everything she had. Removing her engagement ring, she stared at it and fought feeling weepy. Her brain like mush, tears started as she began to brush her teeth. She'd had crying jags in difficult times before, but not lately. She fought it off but by the time she crawled in bed, her boo-hoos had turned into full-blown sobs. There was nothing to do but sleep it off.

The walls were too thick for anybody to hear her. She didn't want Jessica to know and worry about her. If Finn confided in her best friend, she'd come right over, and a still small voice told her she needed to be by herself.

She tossed and turned, the tears streaming down onto her pillow. In the wee hours of the morning, in misery, with a physical ache piercing her heart, she prayed aloud. "Lord, help me. Help me to keep my commitments."

She had to hang onto her sanity most of all.

Chapter Seven

The next morning after the party for Kayla's twins, Clint gazed out over the fields behind his house earlier than usual. The chilled air required a jacket. But signs of spring encouraged him, every green tinge of grass.

The door sprung closed with a smack behind him. "I didn't expect you for another hour." Cam came out onto the porch with him.

"It's surprising how much more I get done when Lilly has a sleepover. I miss her somethin' fierce. Yesterday slipped by without getting much done, what with getting served the legal papers and getting situated with Finn."

He was trying to get used to calling Finn his fiancée. But it felt strange to call her that, especially when Cam knew the truth.

"Let's get started on the chores. We'll talk while we work."

The man was already two steps ahead of Clint, so the idea wasn't optional. Cam didn't have much to say, no matter what. Clint had come to appreciate his silence, and this morning he had thinking of his own to do. He couldn't wait to get started with his breeding horses that was going to be his major contribution to the farm. He'd been learning the ropes a bit and was ready to get down to business.

He shook off the thoughts and took some quick steps to catch up and Bentley, their overgrown Border Collie mix, ran out from nowhere. Clint stopped and scratched the old dog's ears. Cam surprised him by slowing and patting his broad back. His muzzle was nearly all white now. "You sleep in today, boy?"

He let the dog wander off. "I'm not done with the efforts needed to fight Louella's filing, either. I'll help on the farm as much as I can. The lawyer could only schedule a meeting this morning. I'll be having lunch with Finn, too."

Cam cocked an eyebrow. "Why you spending so much time with her, for a fake relationship? Something's going on you're not telling me."

Clint took a swig of coffee from his go cup. Cam only listened to few words, and he wasn't getting into talking about Fin. "Hey, you know I love ya' and I know you're a great catch and deserve to find a wonderful woman. I was surprised yesterday. When I finished talking with Finn, you were gone. Did something happen with Jessica?"

"Nothin'. Thing is, you're spending time with Finn wearing Mom's ring. More going on there than I have with anybody I'd legit like to date. Sort of like to date. I'm out of practice and wasn't that great at it anyway."

His brother had stops and starts with a few women in the past, but Clint wasn't sure if he was serious about settling down. He knew he wasn't going to, not with Lilly as his main concern. Maybe being commitment-shy ran in the family, at the stage of life he and Cam were in anyway.

They arrived at the barn. "You gave the okay on the ring and everybody knows about it. Jessica turned you down?"

"I didn't ask her anything. Hadn't planned to. Visiting wasn't goin' how I wanted so I left."

"Women aren't easy. You know that. We all have dry spells." No truer words had been spoken. Cam's points were valid.

Clint went to Blaze in his stall and let him out first. He'd get out to exercise more as the weather got milder. He checked their food and water. Yesterday's schedule had him cutting corners and he'd make it up today, starting with mucking the stalls. The rugs laid down for comfort on the barn floor needed a good cleaning, and today he wanted to brush the horses more thoroughly.

The time went quickly, and it felt good to work his muscles through labor. Gave him something to do other than think about his problems. Kissing Finn hadn't been in his plans but giving her the ring had touched something he hadn't thought about for a very long time. What started as a nice gesture to give simple thanks had him distracted. He wanted more.

If only this situation wasn't all tangled up with the lawsuit. Finn came across as steady, which he liked and that kept him from worrying she'd make a wrong move. They'd managed okay so far. But meeting today was critical to ironing out some details. He didn't want to do anything that would change her choice to help him.

Clint's phone alarm went off. He neatened up the stall as best he could, hung the pitchfork where it belonged, and waved goodbye to Cam. Guilt threatened to raise its head, but he shoved it down. Chores were endless on a farm. Lilly, his precious daughter, took precedence. They'd hire another person to pick up the slack, if it came to that. The prospect of seeing Finn added to his good spirits.

He cleaned up and put on a special shirt he'd had delivered. He felt better when he dressed well, and this was his brother's attorney he would meet. Caleb had referred him after liking the work he did when Kayla had been in drug rehab and he became the guardian for Drew and Ella. That was before Clint's time here. The Galloways openly shared details of their lives with one another, and they included him.

Now he was keeping a big secret from them all.

Light my path, Lord. Forgive my deception.

By the time he was on the short drive to town, Clint used the few minutes to review what he wanted to say if the attorney took his case. He'd tried to be prepared and searched online for information. If a child was school age, there were ways to present evidence they were doing well. But Lilly was just a baby.

Once he was in the Tate and Tate law office, the preliminary questions were easy. But he wanted to impress upon them how committed he was. He took an opening when they asked if he had questions.

"Lilly's my life. I know sometimes dads get the short stick in court. I'm not perfect. But this is my girl. She belongs with me, and I'll fight for her with everything in my being."

Bill Tate's piercing green eyes looked out above his half glasses. "As your daughter's only living parent, it's a slam dunk you'll get custody under normal circumstances. What's worrying you?"

"Louella is a determined, vindictive woman. She's got some mental problems and losing her daughter sent her over the edge, I believe. I actually feel sorry for her and wish she'd get help. I'm a little worried about her spending time with Lilly. My family and I are public figures, to a certain extent. My name has appeared in the media in unsavory situations. The stories were inaccurate. I anticipate she'll exploit them anyway. I want what's fair to her and to Lilly. She should see Lilly for a short time, right here in Fair Creek, under supervision."

Clint's hands trembled, but it was so mild he thought it must be internal. He shoved the file of clippings over with gusto to cover it up.

"Do you know if any mental issues have been diagnosed?"

Clint leaned back in his chair. He'd never share something so private unless he were up against a wall like this. "Trixie's mother had drastic mood swings that strained our marriage. We joked she must be bipolar. She's wealthy and I didn't know if she was just eccentric."

The man pushed the file back toward Clint. "We have our own methods. I'll take your case. Once I've looked over everything, we'll call and schedule."

Clint opened the file and pulled out a typed sheet he'd created for the meeting. He had Finn's name on it and gave details about their engagement along with her contact information.

Once Clint was out on the street, the sun seemed brighter. His step seemed lighter somehow as he walked to Delaney's to meet Finn. He was ready to put this custody issue behind him. The anticipation of seeing Finn added to his good spirits.

He wouldn't analyze that now.

After checking his watch, he stopped in to Hit the Nail, the little hardware store, to price some items they'd need to start restoring Jessica's building. He liked to buy local and expected to do business right in Fair Creek, though.

The green awning covered in fabric above the front window at Delaney's looked downright jaunty in the sunlight, like the others in a row along Main. The diner windows were painted for Easter. Bunnies and eggs abounded on a green lawn that looked shaped more like the peeks of water in a lake. Finn hadn't arrived and he went to the counter and emptied the change in his pocket into a can. Every penny counted as a vote in the economic growth council's decorating contest for Fair Creek.

At a large round table near the center of the dining room, Ted and Elizabeth sat with other seniors. Ted spotted Clint and his face lit up. "Come see our service project."

Clint headed over just as he glimpsed Finn coming down the sidewalk to enter the diner. "You helping the Easter bunny?" Candy was spread out all over the counter and they were stuffing it into plastic eggs.

"We sure are. Avoiding temptation mainly. These are for the community Easter egg hunt. The days are gone for eating my weight in chocolate." He made a pretend frowning face.

Elizabeth patted her husband's arm. "Blood sugar issues aren't fun, are they?"

Finn came over and surprised him when she slipped her arm around Clint's waist. When she removed it just as unexpectedly, he stopped himself from making a frowning face, too, missing her warmth and connection.

Uh oh. He was in trouble.

"When's the wedding?" Someone he'd met somewhere, Shirley, he thought, had called out the question. This community and his family were a lot of people to remember. Clint felt his heart sink—literally. A part of him wanted to stop this now and the other wanted to joke around.

The story of his life. "We're checking on castles in Ireland. We'll get back with you."

Finn rolled her eyes. "We're taking things slowly." She was on her game today. She grabbed his hand and pulled him far from the other diners, making it seem natural that a couple would want to break away by themselves.

They had a moment when they were alone. "Smooth. You're getting good at this." He'd stop thinking about misleading people and faced facts. He wasn't hurting anybody. Plus, what they were doing would protect his child.

Fin's skin seemed pale as she dropped his hand and went around to a table that was tucked next to one wall. "Over here by ourselves, we can exchange information without anyone noticing.

She pulled out a piece of paper and handed it to him.

It had a list of information to fill in about him. "Uh, well. Let's make it more of an interview, if you don't mind?"

"Oh, sure. I just . . ."

Sierra came to their table. "What cha' having kids? Great party last night, huh?"

They both spoke at once. "The regular."

Sierra tilted her head to one side and chewed on the end of her pen. "How come you guys've never come in together? Probably don't even know you order the same thing."

Clint froze. Finn fumbled with something in her purse.

"Anyway. Gotta take care of my other customers. It's good to see you both."

After she left, Finn pulled out the list she'd given him and scrawled on it, then returned it.

"List your favorite foods" had been added to the end.

She still seemed a bit pale, her hand shaky, and he had to ask. "Everything okay?"

Their two glasses of water came, and she gulped down another drink. "Fine."

"C'mon. You can tell me. We're engaged."

She took another swallow.

Finn gave him the side eye one of his foster mothers used to give him.

"Sorry. For a minute there, I thought we really were special. I do care about you, Finn."

She quirked an eyebrow and looked cuter than ever. If that was even possible. "That's okay. I get mixed up, too. I like spending time with you."

His expression turned serious, with some sort of a shadow passing over his eyes. "Relationship 101, starting by coming clean about something I normally keep to myself. Last night was great. But I sometimes feel a little deflated by those big events, like I don't fit in. None of 'em know what it's like to bounce around in foster care, then find out your father's name later in life. I mean, the first family we were placed with as first graders was a great family of faith. We're forever grateful we were saved but circumstances took us away from them. I love my Galloway brothers. I really do. But they had whole, fulfilling lives, not knowing I existed."

She pulled her glass closer, unwrapped a straw with precision and poked it in her drink before taking a long slow swig. "That hurts my heart, knowing you feel that way. Just so you know, one way to tell I'm nervous is if I'm constantly gulping water."

"Better be careful. I'll take back your drink like I do when Lilly overdoes it," Clint teased. "Ya' know, I always wonder if others feel so low, at times. But nobody talks about this stuff." He looked at the room half full of people. Some were friends, and some family, like Sierra. Leaning forward, he said, "People in this room have their own pain but we'll never know what. And now I've shared mine, and you're basically a stranger."

She looked him in the eye and he couldn't look away. "I beg to differ. We're far from strangers, Clint. If it makes you feel better, you've given me courage to share my truth, too." Finn straightened her shoulders. "I thought I could do this fake fiancée thing. But last night made me wonder. Strange how our thoughts that drag us back to hard times aren't that different, yours and mine. We can have a great time, and it also might bring back memories that make us sad, or make us realize something's missing, all at the same time."

She had his full attention, and he stopped himself from interrupting as she continued. "I'll rip the cover off, like we do returned books we can't sell. When I was 17, I went to junior prom at my high school. We were on a blind date. He forced himself on me. I had a baby I gave up for adoption."

Her lip quivered for a second. She was so brave. "Thinking of not knowing Lilly, and you giving up your baby. The pain of that wouldn't be something I'd get over easily. You okay?"

She nodded slowly up and down. Her blue eyes shimmered with unshed tears.

Sierra swung by their table and placed their plates in front of them. "Eat up, kids."

Finn and Clint's eyes locked and she giggled. "Now, you know I like sardines on my burger, right, Sierra?"

Clint looked at his burger and made a face. "I better not've gotten yours. Now I'm scared to lift the bun."

Sierra tucked her pen behind her ear. She tossed up her hands. "You guys are pulling my leg."

Clint said, "Just remembered, you weren't working when I came in and changed my regular to anchovies on top."

With hands on her hips, Sierra gave a sassy twist of her head. "I'm not sure what you're pulling here. But you guys aren't very good at fooling people. Now, you both have lettuce, tomato and mayo like you ordered. Finn, I'll bring you another glass of water. Now, I've gotta get back to my honest customers." She stomped off, obviously making a show because she didn't get mad often.

Finn shrugged. "This whole situation must be stressing us out. We're losing it, a little bit."

"I don't know what we're doing. But I'm honored you shared your story with me. Getting to know you is a good thing that's come out of having my former mother-in-law trying to get custody of Lilly."

Finn patted his hand, then pulled back from how he made her feel, all warm and a bit clingy. "I can't be crushing on my fake fiancé now, can I?" She picked up a fry and a bottle of catsup, then slowly squirted a perfect line along the fry. She ate it, savoring every bite. Sierra brought her glass of water and she guzzled down another a drink.

Clint finished off his burger and his fries were long gone. "What I know is that I don't want to hurt you, and I won't make you go through with this."

"I said I wondered if I could do this. I didn't say I was calling it off."

Chapter Eight

Finn strolled down Main Street on her way to open Wind in the Willows, determined to appear she didn't have a care in the world. People said to fake it 'til you make it. Even pretend smiles supposedly made a person feel more like smiling, for real.

She needed this theory to work—badly.

As she went by the Main Street boutique storefronts, she judged the Easter themes painted on the windows of each one. Every year, the competition for the prettiest became more intense —and cut-throat. The Lone Mum's spectacular display couldn't be beat. If the florist shop hadn't won the last two years, she'd have chosen theirs. Besides painting on green grass to look signal spring, their animated mechanical bunnies stood taller than Leo Galloway, whom she'd just met last night. Live plants were arranged on the ground all around. Fin stopped and went closer. She was pretty sure those bunnies had escaped their burrow and attended last night's Galloway Sons Farm birthday party.

With the memory, her smile started to falter. Birthdays were reminders of years gone by. Her baby she'd given up when she was seventeen would be an adult now. Her cheeks flushed thinking about how she'd overshared with Clint earlier. At least she'd stopped herself from crying, just barely.

She picked up her speed as she went by Vintage Finds with its giant paper mâché mama sheep. Live baby lambs, with white fuzzy fur, were scampering around. The insides of their ears showed a bright pink. Patton Farms hauled them into town six days a week until Easter. Contest rules didn't allow anything that breathed so they were disqualified from the town decorating contest.

One tiny glimpse of the fluffy little darlings soothed Finn's aching heart somewhat. She wasn't a rule-breaker by nature though and wouldn't vote for Vintage Finds.

A little girl with her mother stood staring and pointing. "Love your matching dresses, ladies," Finn called out as she passed by. In identical pink checked gingham dresses, each wore a jumbo hair bow. Nellie from Little House on the Prairie reruns, which she'd watched with Grandma Patterson, had nothing on them.

"I want a lamby, Mommy. Mommy!" The lambs were so popular, no one wanted to lower the boom on Lonny, the Vintage Find's store owner to stop them.

Maybe Lilly would whine when *she* got older.

Would Finn even know the little girl when she was that age? The question tugged at her heartstrings.

Finn moved on and went by Hit the Nail, which featured a primitive vibe of green grass growing up the side of a hill, and a gigantic cross at the top. She waved to the owner, amazed at the story of how he'd formed the cross from two huge nails, and put a crown of thorns where they crisscrossed. She shot up a little prayer, like she did every day. She wanted Easter to bring renewal for her this year.

"Great seeing you last night. Congrats again on your engagement!" Abby stood outside The Melody Shop. She shook a rug, dust flying.

"Thank you! We enjoyed the little music makers!"

Abby seemed to lean on the side of the building for support. "I just got the call two of my singers for the Easter cantata are sick. Do you sing?"

She didn't want to answer. But there'd be no more lies for her, she'd decided. "Yes, but not well. In the shower, mostly."

"The point of a special Easter choir show is to enjoy the music and make a joyful noise. God handles the rest. Just think about it, okay?"

"I'm sure the right people will come along." Finn pressed her lips together so she wouldn't volunteer, then started walking. She'd be late if she kept this up, so she quit looking at storefronts until she reached her own, the door she shared with Jessica's bakery.

The stuffed bunny she'd attached to the light pole pleased her more than it should. She wouldn't win and hadn't even entered. Her heart swelled that she'd contributed to beautifying the town. Maybe she'd find someone to paint her window, too.

Finn pushed open the shop door that was already unlocked. On Wednesdays, Jessica opened in the morning and covered for her until she came in the afternoon.

The bell over the door jangled and she admired the smiley-faced pot Clint had given her for the entry. By the time Finn had weeded out some dead leaves and entered the inner circle, Jessica was there waiting.

Finn stowed her purse under a nearby counter. "What's up?"

With sparkling eyes and a huge grin on her face, Jessica grabbed Finn's hand. "How's my favorite bibliophile? Look what I have!"

Papers held together by paperclips, like she'd requested, could mean one thing. "More essays people brought in?!" She did a quick count of the papers. "Nine, to put with the others. I'd half-forgotten today's the last day to enter for the chance to get into the Easter anthology."

Jessica's smile reminded Finn of the Cheshire Cat from *Alice's Adventures in Wonderland*. "Oh, and somebody came in and bought that trilogy with the fancy cover and the painted edges, whatever you call it."

"That's a special edition. I bought them for people like me, who like extra pretty copies of their favorite books, that look nice on their shelves."

This news, of the sales and the essays, was so affirming. Finn grabbed a tissue from the box in the children's nook, worried she'd burst into tears. Horrified, she fled toward the back rooms.

What was wrong with her?

Her scurrying landed her by the bathroom. She walked in and peered into the vintage oval mirror. She'd always loved its ornate gold trim and how it hung over the antique pedestal sink.

Jessica poked her head in the open doorway. "What's going on with you?"

"I wish I knew. You'd be the first one I'd tell. But really, last night I cried like my heart was breaking. I wasn't going to say anything, but—"

"Of course you should tell me!" Jessica hung her head. "I wish I could help, but you know I'm not the best with emotions. Do you think maybe you just needed a good cry?"

"Okayyyy. You're going to make me go there. Memories popped up last night when I was with Clint and Lilly at the kids' party, and I didn't know how to deal. But you selling those books for me and people turning in the essays had a similar impact on my emotions. It's crazy."

I'm crazy.

Jessica gave her a long hug. "You were practically a kid when incredibly hard stuff happened to you. Maybe you never processed it. Hey, take as long as you need in here."

She seemed to lean between going back to the store and staying with her, when Finn found words. "You know how I hate mental math. Well, yesterday Emily would've turned 19. Doesn't seem that long since we had our painful goodbye."

Jessica let a tear fall that Finn didn't have in her. "I used to call Grandma Patterson all the time, to find out how you were doing. You've always had bigger emotions than I have, and I just don't always know how to help. As upset as I was that you were living across the country and having a baby, I knew you must be losing it. Sometimes I think I'm not the kind of friend you need."

Finn hugged Jessica and then she just held on. "I don't think I can let go. You'll have to pry my cold dead hands from you."

Jessica pulled away and Finn looked up. "And sometimes, you're just a total goofball, and I think we're twins from another mother."

The door out front jingled and Jessica turned serious. "If I answer that, will you be okay?"

"Now that we've talked, I will be."

She scurried out to the public area full of what they both truly loved, the baked goods and the books.

Finn lingered in the back, not quite believing Clint and his brothers would start the building repairs soon. She wasn't sure why she was so excited. Getting the work done for free would be great. But she'd never been into anything associated with buildings before, so this was new. The whole process should be interesting, and a great way to get to know Clint better. She really wanted to.

Don't think about why.

Coming from a family that had so many challenges, as an only child with a single mom, Finn hadn't ever had the chance to see siblings work together. Clint had a twin, and his life hadn't been easy, either. Maybe she'd been wrong that having the brother or sister she'd wanted as a child would have made all the difference. She was looking forward to seeing the Galloway family interactions though.

Hunting through a cabinet, she found her lip gloss that a make-up artist had chosen to enhance the shade of her hair. After a quick swipe, she tested out some smiles by looking at herself in the mirror. "Fake it till you make it," she said. Then she threw her head back and tried to laugh like Clint. But he wasn't easily imitated and she didn't delve into the reason why she'd wanted to. Could you miss someone deeply you'd just met?

Not entirely successful, she'd perked herself up enough to face the world when Jessica reappeared. "Someone's here to see you. I get the feeling she didn't want to tell me her name. Maybe that was in case you weren't here." She shrugged.

Finn followed Jessica into the business part but veered off into Wind in the Willows. Kayla Galloway stood looking through the children's book section. Not sure why Kayla came, Finn pulled out a couple of children's books from behind a counter, putting herself in her comfort zone.

She went over to the Galloway sister. "It's nice to see you, Kayla. In case you're interested, here's a great read for Ella and Drew. It's the most popular book for three-year-olds on the bestseller lists."

Kayla stepped back from the bookshelf. "Oh, I just thought I'd come by and say hi. Hope that's okay."

Finn lowered the book down by her side. "Sure, come any time. Bring the kids. Actually, I'm having a children's story time tomorrow."

Kayla went to a corner by the window where Finn had put small storybooks about a bunny, with matching mini stuffed animals nearby. Kayla grabbed two books and two stuffed animals. "Oh, I have to have these. Thanks for the invite tomorrow. Drew and Ella both love books. They're completely different personalities, though, even being twins. These are for Ella and her friend."

Really. Maybe Finn was taking the wrong approach to getting her children's books off the ground. She'd only read the library association's tips, not getting into what personalities liked what. It was split up by age groups and other categories.

She went over. "I would imagine a boy and a girl might have different interests. Hope they enjoyed their birthday."

"They did, without a doubt. Seems like they're still on the sugar roller coaster ride or maybe just wound up."

Finn put the book in her hand down on a bookshelf for later and picked up a little holder of bright-colored bookmarks for kids.

"Here, you can pick out one of these for each of them that suits their interests. I give them away to kids."

Kayla shook her head. "Thanks for the offer but Drew would destroy one of those."

Finn frowned but quickly schooled her face to smile like she'd seen teachers do. "Well. some of them are scratch-and-sniff, and some kids like strawberry." According to the library association.

"Oh no! I wouldn't put it past Ella to munch on one."

Finn pulled the dispenser away and returned it to the shelf. What could the library association possibly know anyway? Her eyes were drawn to the bath time books, and she held out the basket full of them. "Do they read in the bathtub?"

Kayla stopped looking over the nooks and crannies. "They love bath time and I haven't tried that. Give me two of your favorites."

"Great!"

She picked one about farm animals and another with objects on each page, then went to the counter and Kayla followed. Finn put hers on the counter and Kayla did, too, then said, "I hoped to talk with you."

Finn's jaw clenched. She'd thought they were talking already. But she was supposed to be the fiancée, so it seemed to make sense to chat more. Maybe they'd be friends after all this. But wait, she and Clint were headed toward a bad break-up.

Everything was starting to make her head spin. *You're doing this for Lilly . . .and Emily."*

She stepped over to where two upholstered reading chairs were near a table. "Let's pull these closer together, out of the center." Tension in Finn's shoulders grew. Hopefully, Kayla would be easy to talk to, nothing too serious.

Kayla took the seat across from her. "Last night you seemed a little uneasy around the kids."

Finn registered a pain in the pit of her stomach. "I haven't spent any time around children, if that's what you mean."

There, she didn't sound defensive at all. Right?

Her words hadn't phased Kayla, though. "I'm not sure if you know I was addicted to drugs so bad I lost custody of my kids. My brother, Caleb, took the twins in, with a whole lot of help from Annie. This was before they were married."

Something soft was in Finn's hands but she was too absorbed in the conversation to look. Now, she dropped her gaze. The tissue she'd gotten in case she cried lay shredded like confetti in her lap. She stuffed it into her pocket.

Confessions from other people always made her feel she had to spill her secrets. This was as good a time and place as any. "I know nothing about your situation. My only experience with children was my prom date forcing himself on me and ending up pregnant."

"Oh my word. Did you press charges? I'm so sorry."

It hit Finn that Kayla was like the other Galloways, from what she'd seen. They had good hearts, especially for children.

"It's okay. I'm thirty-six now. Going to the police wasn't something I could face. I came from the wrong side of the tracks. My best friend, she came and got me. She's over there running The Sweet Shop bakery. Her grandma let me come and live with her until I had Emily. Everybody assumed I'd give her up for adoption. At the time, I was pressured into a closed adoption. I was pretty crushed down by life at that point and didn't put up a fight." Even with Mom being gone five years, loyalty made her hold back from telling Kayla how her mother had badgered her to give up her baby.

The bell above the door jingled. Finn hopped up, never so excited to have a conversation interrupted. "Just a minute. I'll be back." Shirley Leap owned Beadangled, the local beading store, and stepped in with her daughter Amelia.

Finn patted the girl's arm. "You're only thirteen and taller than me?"

Amelia smiled, flashing a mouth full of braces, and Shirley handed Finn some papers. "Shot up like a string bean. I can't keep her in clothes. Those are our Easter essays. We had fun."

Amelia rolled her eyes and flipped her blonde, curly hair just like her mom's, except it went all the way down her back. "She bribed me."

"I most certainly did not!" Shirley grinned at Finn. "I've gotta get to a class and she's getting picked up for basketball practice."

They hustled out and Finn had no choice but to walk toward the chairs to pick up her hard conversation. "Sorry about that." She slid back into her seat.

Kayla nodded. "I just wanted to say we have something in common. We have heavy hearts over our children."

Her throat closed up at Kayla's words. "Would you like something to drink? Water or coffee? I've got a mini fridge in the back. Oh, and how are we alike exactly, other than having had kids, I mean?" She didn't want to bother Jessica in the bakery for the drinks. It was still hard for Finn to process she'd given birth to a child and didn't have one anymore.

"I'm not thirsty. Besides, I'll need to go pick up the kids soon. Through our own decisions, we lost our children. It's a burden to bear. I lost my kids for a while. Their dad died of an overdose. They could've been orphans because of me. You were young and I'm not judging you. But I'd be surprised if you have no regrets over giving up Emily."

Finn let out a sigh. It got easier to talk about the more she did it. "You're right. I do."

Kayla covered Finn's hand with hers for a moment, then stood. "For me, the hardest thing is to forgive myself. I believe God's forgiven me. One day, I'll ask for my kids' forgiveness."

Would Finn ever have the chance to speak with Emily?

Kayla gathered her bag and slung it over her shoulder and Finn settled on how much to share. "Mine turned out to be my only chance to have a baby and I failed her. Her name's Emily." Naming her was respectful, but it felt a little like stabbing her own heart. Admitting out loud she wouldn't ever be a mom made it real, not in a good way.

Kayla sat back down dropped her bags by the chair. "Oh, you

never know the future, with you and Clint. . . .I'm texting Bree to see if she'll pick up Drew and Ella so I'll have a couple minutes longer. She couldn't be at the party so you didn't meet her. She's married to my brother, Gage, and they just got back from out of town. She's pregnant."

Kayla wanted to help, but she and Clint didn't have a future. Besides, if she had been in a real engagement, Finn would have been around oodles of Galloway babies. She didn't think she was ready for that.

She could use a drink about now. "I'll need to write down all your brothers' names on my palm to keep 'em straight."

Kayla laughed, and Finn recognized a hint of Clint in her facial expression. "I won't argue that. Let me finish, okay? Finn, the Bible's full of what most people'd call failures. I wouldn't be talking to you right now if I hadn't been in this position. Our struggles bring us together. It's hard. It really is. But it's our mistakes that make us the most helpful to other people. I'm here to give a lifeline because someone gave one to me. Caleb came to my rescue and Annie right along with him. Jesus, too."

"You've given me something to think about. I'm glad you came by. I've gotta get going. Tomorrow's my first story time and I'll learn from it and probably make some changes. If you can't come, I hope you try some other time. And if a group doesn't seem doable, we could set a time, and I'll read with them by themselves to see how it goes."

What was she getting herself into? She'd never read to one child.

The door jingled and in a couple of seconds, Clint stepped in and over where they were. For today, she wished she could shut off the tinkling bell. It was exhausting.

Finn hopped up and went to great him, with energy she hadn't known she had. A belt around his waist had tools hanging from it and he carried a long tool. She thought about kissing him —only for fake fiancée purposes. But it seemed like the break-up would just be harder if they did. She shoved down a sadness from nowhere. "Speaking of a carpenter, here you are."

A slight red shade climbed up Clint's cheeks. "I'm not a carpenter, more like a handyman."

"Oh. Are you thinking if I were a good little fiancée, I'd know your trade? No worries. Me and Kayla were actually talking about Jesus, the ultimate carpenter."

Clint gave her that smile that was growing on her, and maybe had a slight dimple thrown in. "I don't think anyone could ever mix me up with Jesus."

Finn offered him a bottled water Jessica handed her. "It might take a special toolbox. I love you anyway." She swallowed. She'd broken rule. Maybe that's why his eyes lit up. She talked on, unaware of the words coming out of her mouth. Surely he knew she was teasing. Wasn't she? "If you're working here, we'll be getting to see you every day. Hey, you like bottled water or not?"

It seemed everything she said hinted she didn't really know Clint. But Kayla was the only one who might notice because she seemed to pay attention and was getting to know them both.

But seeing she was distracted, Jessica had rung up Kayla's order, including two superheroes pens added to her stash, so she was on her way out anyway. "Thanks for stopping in." That seemed wholly inadequate for that conversation but what could you do? Sometimes, there really were no words. But she certainly loved trying to find some. Words had enthralled her when she was a girl, from the minute she spelled "fox." Her mom had been at her best, before everything went wrong.

Clint had walked to the far wall and returned, waving off the water, likely clueless that an important conversation had just happened for her. "You were gone somewhere, there for a minute," he said. "I'm just cruising in to use my handy dandy level because Leo's offered his paintings for your walls. How's that sound? Masterpieces deserve to hang *straight*. That's my artist brother, if I didn't tell you."

"You didn't and I'm wondering if we're really engaged at all," she teased.

With his level in one hand, as he called it, so he didn't hit his toolbelt on his hip, he came closer. "I have to pinch myself sometimes to believe you're engaged to be mine."

She thought she might melt into a puddle. But they were pretending, right?

His hand tugged her along then released her. "Now, will you come over here and show me your best places for the art? You might get tired of me since I'll be around so much."

Somehow, Finn didn't think so.

Chapter Nine

C lint lay in his bed and enjoyed the quiet of the night. That was true even if it was two thirty a.m. and he wanted to have dropped off and gone back to sleep. He and Cam had lived in various cities in the state of Tennessee. Coming here to Indiana had been a change, for the better.

He'd left curtains off one of the windows in his loft bedroom intentionally. He'd never have had the luxury when he lived in town.

At times like right now, he looked directly out at the night sky. When he'd gone to bed earlier, he'd fallen asleep gazing at the stars twinkling overhead.

His phone dinged telling him he had a text message. He'd forgotten to silence it as he normally did. The phone clock said three o'clock a.m.

It was from Finn Moore. "Hi, I know you won't get this until morning, but I didn't want to forget. Today's toddler story time at Wind in the Willows. Hope Lilly can come. With your farm work and all you have going on, let me know if I can help get Lilly."

He replied: Hi, Hopefully, you're not sleepless in Fair Creek like I am. Thank you for thinking of us. We'll be at story time and use our own transport. Looking forward to more "engagement" with you. He ended with a smiley emoji.

Being in touch with someone at this time of night, even if it was digitally, lifted his mood. Or maybe interacting with Finn boosted him, at any time.

Wherever they'd lived before, there had been no such thing as this quiet. At times, it unnerved Clint. Some noise was always happening somewhere. It could be loud or soft, but quiet had been hard to come by. He and Trixie had lived in Nashville, but she'd never seemed impacted by noise or light.

A sharp cry sounded on the baby monitor. He threw the covers off his legs and went to Lilly's room next to his. A dim light came from underneath the closet door where a night light stayed on all night. She stood in her crib, her eyes nearly closed. They looked like slits, her lids were so close to being shut.

Clint wrapped her in a hug, hoping to get her back to sleep without them both fully coming awake. It was probably too late for him to get a good night's sleep, but Lilly had a chance. Her body seemed to relax in his arms as they both stood there. He just needed to be careful he didn't get so relaxed he fell or something. The delicate scents of her lotion and her shampoo wafted up. He inhaled. Until she moved in, he didn't get why people said parenting changed them.

Lilly's breathing evened out and became so deep he knew she was asleep. Now came the test. He knew from experience that not letting her stay asleep long enough made her wake up when he left.

To keep track of time, he counted in his head. '*One Mississippi. Two Mississippi. Three Mississippi.*" When he'd measured enough seconds to equal two minutes, he should be able to leave, if all went well.

This counting and the quiet were putting him back to sleep. Carefully, like dealing with a bomb that might have its wire tripped, he lifted her and stretched her out on her back. Clint stood at her bed as a safety measure. If putting her down didn't "take," he would repeat the process again.

When she first came to stay with him, people assumed he was sleep deprived. But then he told them she slept through the night, and they'd let him know she was a "good sleeper."

He'd liked the dark and the quiet. But since he'd been handed the custody papers, he sometimes craved sound and light, so he didn't have to think. He'd also stopped being able to sleep through the night, no matter how tired he was.

Lilly was securely in dreamland, and he crawled back into his bed, ready for more sleep himself.

Morning came too soon for both of them. His alarm clock didn't normally go off since Lilly was usually up by six a.m. He didn't like to wake her up, but she had a schedule today. Taking her to storytelling with Finn would be fun for her. She curled up in a little ball and then took a big stretch in her crib. By the time he picked her up and had her on the changing table, she gave him a little grin.

"We were up late last night, weren't we?"

She just followed what he was doing with her eyes. She had a sunny attitude most of the time, and he was grateful. It made life easier—for both of them. He hoped she never lost that.

He remembered having a grouchy attitude in junior high. That age had been hard enough without him and Cam being placed with a foster family they didn't feel compatible with. It wasn't an abuse situation but had been neglect. They'd fended for themselves and leaned on a school counselor, sometimes to get them food to fill their stomachs. Other times they'd receive better fitting coats or shoes that didn't pinch their toes. But Cam had always had his back, even then. He put Clint ahead when there wasn't enough for them both. They'd made it through together until getting reassigned.

If he lost custody, Lilly would be all alone to face changes. Trixie's mother would not be a role model, either. In her early 50s, she'd been a young mother, and possibly wanted another chance to raise a child? He hoped to avoid making bipolar tendencies an issue but she made decisions without much thought. He couldn't stand the idea of any of it, not for his darling Lilly.

Would it just be him and Lilly in ten-plus years? Since the terrible marriage he'd had with Trixie, it was fine if doing that again passed him by. She'd been eight years younger, and his ex-wife had been beautiful, on the outside, but misguided. With only a string of foster families as his role models, he'd been at a loss about what to look for in a relationship. For a rising photographer at the level he'd been, and making a fortune, appearances mattered.

But a little girl needed a woman. Lilly was blessed with a multitude of aunts, which would have to do.

He didn't think he needed a woman for himself but spending time with Finn had been better than he thought possible. He couldn't wait to see her today, to see her smile and maybe have a laugh.

He'd tossed Lilly's diaper in the bin and put a new one on her, while she gurgled and squirmed like she was still stretching herself awake. "Your Aunt Annie's coming to pick you up today, so daddy doesn't have to drive you. After I work this morning, we'll be going to see Finn at story time, okay?"

"Nnn."

"Good!"

He'd never been a morning person. It took some real effort to keep up chatting with her like the doctor said to do. He'd read all the books, and that's what they said, too. You were supposed to let little ones hear lots of words.

"I'm leaving you in your PJs. How does that sound? Huh? Do you want to stay warm and cozy a while longer?"

A thought about Finn ran through Clint's head. That happened more and more lately. Taking care of Lilly was his main interest. But now that Finn was in their lives, he automatically thought about them as a couple, at times. Just needing to include her so people believed she was his fiancée had tricked his brain into believing it.

He zipped up Lilly's jammies almost to her chin and sat her in her bouncy seat. It took him an extra several seconds to get the little safety strap snapped up around her. He didn't like to take shortcuts. He was too uncertain about everything to leave the strap thing undone.

The urge to talk about Finn with Lilly came over him. He wasn't sure how much she understood what he said. Parenting articles and books seemed to disagree about everything. If he were to guess, he'd say she knew everything, like some information he'd read said. Her eyes told him she didn't miss a thing.

He patted his daughter's tummy again. "Do you ever wonder what it'd be like if Finny really was your new mommy?" Drool pooled in her mouth and started to spill over onto her front. He got the teether shaped like a sheep out of the basket and gave it to her. She really had a strong grip with her teeth. He didn't know what that type of talent would do for her, but if hanging onto something in your teeth were an Olympic sport, she'd get a gold medal.

"Sometimes I'd like more people here. Maybe Finn could tell me if putting the stuff that numbs your gums on you would be good to use. I can only read conflicting opinions for so long. Daddies don't know everything."

"Dadd. Dadada."

"She doesn't know as much about kids as I do, though. We could help her learn, right?"

He patted Lilly's tummy and sort of half tickled her. She giggled. In her fuzzy pajamas with the feet in them with bunnies all over, she looked especially cute.

"You're going to be a heartbreaker one day, ya know that?"

He threw it into high gear and started tossing in what she'd need for the day into her diaper bag. Should've done it last night. But he couldn't keep ahead of everything.

There was a knock on the front door just as he finished up.

He'd gotten himself up and ready for the day before she woke up. That's one thing he'd learned.

When he got them both together, he saw Cam had already let Annie in. He might have called her an angel multiple times when she picked up Lilly's things and he carried her out in her car seat.

"This feels like such a luxury for you to do this. Thanks."

"You're welcome. It must be really hard doing everything all on your own."

"Yeah, it's okay."

"Think of it this way. You'll only be on your own for a while longer. Then you'll have Finn to help. We're all just so happy for you."

She didn't seem to notice he didn't say anything to that. The way she described it sounded nice. He told himself he couldn't lose something he never had though.

He waved goodbye and after grabbing his coffee, Clint trudged out to the barn, feeling the caffeine kick in as he went. Could it happen that quickly? It was another thing to read up on.

"You look like something Bentley dragged in."

"Nah, some of those mice he catches look better than me."

Clint patted Blaze and counted to ten, considering whether to bring up a topic bothering him. He was doing way too much counting lately but sometimes waiting was the best form of action. He opened the horse's stall and patted his rump as he went out for some exercise.

"Thanks for getting the door when Annie knocked. Lilly and I were moving slower than usual. Hey, can I ask you something?"

Cam headed toward the area to check the feed. "Sure. We should be able to talk about anything."

"Some people are still talking about the meeting on solar energy for farms a few months back."

Cam stopped what he was doing. "Who's sayin' what?"

Clint grabbed a pitchfork and started working in Blaze's stall, trying to keep it casual. "I'm not sure if the details matter. You know there's strong opinions on both sides. That includes in our own family."

Cam stood fuming and Clint half expected steam to spurt from his ears. "So tell me something I don't know."

After stabbing the pitchfork into the ground, Clint leaned on it. "I can't think of anything. But as CEO of Vortex Clean Energy, Wyatt didn't appreciate his half-brother, that he considers his brother, opposing him in public."

Cam removed his hat and ran his fingers through his hair. "I had valid reasons for my views. Are you bringing this up because Wyatt said something to you?

Holding himself back from removing his own hat, Clint mulled over that having similar habits wasn't always pleasant. "Gimme a break. I'm trying to avoid a food fight at the next kids' birthday party. I saw you guys avoiding each other at Drew and Ella's party."

"It wasn't that bad."

Clint stopped his work and faced Cam with the gate in between. "Here's the thing. It was a town meeting. Wyatt is the Galloway son who found out Dad had two sons he didn't know about. He brought you and me into this family." Clint choked up for a second, unable to speak, then went on. "There were plenty of people there that night on both sides. What purpose did it serve for you to speak against Wyatt's company, and Miles, our cousin who helped start the company had come in from out-of-town, too!" He hadn't meant to raise his voice.

"Point taken. What I really wish is that everybody around here wasn't at each other's throats about the pros and cons of solar energy. The yard signs with a mark through solar hurt me to see—the side I'm on—as much as the ones supporting solar. The strained relationships caused by people having differing opinions is a shame. I've done a lot of reading and that's why I gave a public opinion on Wyatt's solar company. I didn't support him, but it wasn't personal. Really, I think farmers oughta be able to use their land as they see fit. Now, I gotta get some work done."

"Cam, look at me. Loyalty. This was about loyalty. You weren't going to change anybody's mind about solar panels. You didn't have to take a public stance because others had already done that. But you've damaged the bonds of this family."

The space in between them was expanding as Cam walked away. Whether physically or emotionally, it felt like Cam walked away too much.

He had to nearly shout for Cam to hear him, not that he appeared to want to. "They're not perfect. But they've been mighty good to us."

Cam got to a feed trough a ways out and threw something in it, oats he figured. "We've been good to them, too. Family shouldn't mean a person can't have their own opinions."

"I reckon you've got a point. Thanks for coming to my Ted Talk."

Cam kept taking care of the chores and so did Clint. They worked in silence. Cam topped off the water supply for the animals, and he seemed to be moving a little more slowly too. "You better not be going out like you used to do. That's not why you're dragging, is it? Cause with that custody case..."

"You know me better than that. Lilly had me up last night. I'm not sleeping well anyway, either, so it's a double whammy."

When he was done mucking stalls, Clint brought two horses back in. He methodically gave them each a good grooming. With each stroke he worked through the whole solar panel fiasco in his head. He'd promised himself to brush the horses and kept putting it off. He'd given them the royal treatment this time.

Cam came back around. "Sorry. I shouldn't be giving you a hard time. I don't think there's much more important in life than kids, after our faith. You'll be relieved when the case is closed and Lilly's yours. Can't happen soon enough."

"Hold that thought."

"I always have. Let me know if there's anything I can do."

"My attorney's organizing character witnesses. You know me

better than anybody. You're living with us so you can attest to the day-to-day."

"I'll do whatever you need. Just let me know. I'll write you the most supportive witness statement ever."

Clint slapped Cam on the back. "I knew I could count on you." And he needed to start acting like he believed that.

Clint finished, and got himself cleaned up, interested to get on to the rest of his day. He didn't mind chores. But lately he had so much more on his mind. Things were just different.

Not all of them had to do with the lawsuit, either.

Chapter Ten

Clint pulled up to the curb on Main Street at the far end of town and shut off the truck. Lilly let out a chirp. He was pretty sure she'd dropped back asleep, based on that sound. He couldn't wait for her to be able to ride in a front-facing car seat so he could see her. But that would be a while, and he didn't want to wish her life away.

He dialed Tate & Tate's number and someone picked up. "Clint Galloway, returning Bill's call."

They put him through, and Bill's voice came on. "I'm headed to court in a few minutes. Here's the edited version, the case brief, as we call it. Your background check isn't bad and it's quite good, actually. The mention of your use of drugs, even casually referenced in the media, isn't in your favor. Oh, and you're being followed."

He took in a breath. This was getting real. "I would've thought I'd notice something."

"We're not in a detective movie."

"Being the subject of a stake-out sounds exciting. They can do that without my consent?"

"Unfortunately, yes. Look, getting your former mother-in-law off your tail, literally, is all that will excite me, as you've phrased it.

Our court date is a week from Wednesday. My paralegal will work with you on the character references. Be sure your fiancée attends. Any questions?"

"Can you help find someone who was in a closed adoption?"

"Yes. My assistant will email you what's needed. Now I really must go."

Clint opened his door and Lilly did another chirp.

"Almost story time, Lilly-Bear!"

Maybe the shut-eye had done her good. She'd fallen asleep right after he picked her up from Annie's. If only he were able to sleep so easily.

He got out and went to the truck bed and unloaded Lilly's red wagon. Being outside was good for her and he found it relaxing. Strollers didn't suit him. Lilly was cooler than that, and so was Clint.

Picking up his little girl from her car seat, he inhaled her scent mixed with a faint lingering of apples. "Did Annie give you apple sauce again?"

She nodded her head up and down. "App sos."

Was he in the *Groundhog Day* movie? It seemed like it, when he said the same things over and over with Lilly. Some might find it boring, or tedious. For some reason he couldn't quite fathom, he didn't. He took it seriously that he was helping with her language skills. What could be more important?

Wearing a little pink, flowered jumpsuit picked out by Annie, Lilly was basically in shorts. He was afraid she might get chilly. After removing the pillows he kept for this purpose from their protective sleeves, he piled them in the bottom of the wagon. They created the perfect padding, and he lifted her up over the side and seated her inside. He wrapped a blanket around her all the way down her legs, to her white shoes and lace anklets. After tying her floppy white bucket hat under her chin, he pulled her along in the wagon toward Wind in the Willows book shop.

The sun had come out and nothing could hold back his good spirits. Clint pulled his shades from his shirt pocket and put them on. He went at a slow pace so Lilly could enjoy the Easter paintings on the storefront windows as they went. At the bookstore, he entered the little entryway after he got the wagon's wheels to go over the door jam.

He pointed up high on the wall loaded with plants. "Daddy gave Mo—" He stopped himself from calling Finn mommy, not to confuse Lilly or freak out Finn. "Daddy gave Finny that little pot, Lilly-Bear." But her head might have been on a swivel, with how she looked at everything. She plucked off a low leaf that looked perfectly green to him. Oops. "Here, let me carry that in my pocket."

Hopefully, destroying plants wasn't the gateway activity of a child headed for juvenile delinquency.

He'd aimed to get here early so he could have some private time with Finn. When he went into the store, she came rushing toward him and gave him a peck on the lips. "You've got to wear those aviator sunglasses more often. I was watching for you from the window." She squatted down to Lilly's level in her wagon. "I'm thrilled you hugged my bunny on the light post, Lilly!"

His daughter showed her most angelic smile, then handed Finn a perfect leaf she'd pulled from one of her plants.

Clint hugged Finn and spun her around once, hoping she'd forget about the leaf. "Count on me wearing those shades every day, if it brings that kind of response from you." He wasn't sure if it was good that this was all becoming more and more natural. He vowed to stop worrying about it and give it to God.

One thing he knew for sure. He was glad he'd come. "Being engaged is the most fun ever. I love... it."

Finn threw her head back and laughed. Clint was taken by how her magnificent hair swirled around her shoulders.

She pointed her finger at him. "The l-word was borderline usage of 'love.' I won't put you in the penalty box this time. I'll admit being engaged with *you* is keeping me entertained."

Had she been engaged to someone else? Maybe he was reading too much into her remark but he didn't like to think that she'd had a serious relationship before. She was a beautiful woman, and she wasn't his and never would be, though. A little of his happiness flitted away.

He was enjoying himself partly because there were parameters, too. He couldn't go too far with her, which protected his heart. But sometimes it felt very real, like they were falling in love. Today was one of those days.

Jessica caught their attention from behind the bakery counter and waved. Several seconds later, she came over with a round, flat cake as big as a pizza, that she'd decorated herself. She'd written in cursive using icing, "We put a ring on it!" Below that, in the outline of a heart she'd written, "Clint & Finn."

Finn spoke in almost a shout as more people came. "You shouldn't have!"

The wood floors and high ceilings didn't help people hear each other, either. He'd love working on this old place, and maybe they could add something to help with acoustics.

"I absolutely should have, and I did." Jessica pulled a phone out of her apron and snapped shots of Clint and Finn standing behind the cake. "This'll be your engagement announcement in the *Gazette*."

Finn nodded. "Be sure to put us on the front page. We need an entertaining description of and how we met, too."

Jessica laughed and laughed. "Make it at a pig wrestling match or donkey basketball game, something like that. I crack myself up sometimes."

Clint was starting to see how the women were friends, even though they were so different. Their quirks seemed to complement one another.

He held up his hands and formed the universal heart shape. "You're the best, Jessica! Now, let me get you ladies' picture with the cake."

"No," they both answered at once.

"Come on. Someday when Finn and I are retired to our rocking chairs, we'll have this memory."

They both laughed a little, but they sounded more nervous than anything. He wondered if they were thinking what he was, that old age and rocking chairs weren't in their plans. "At least I've got a picture with big grins on your faces," he said. Jessica hugged Finn and put the cake on the table with the rest of the refreshments.

More people were starting to gather, mostly mothers with small children in tow. Maybe a few were grandmothers and grandkids.

Finn's wide mile said it all. Clint was glad she seemed to be enjoying herself in their pretend engagement. "I've had the essays edited and the booklet formatted. I'm ready for the cover photo with Lilly and the chicks."

He found the best photo and texted it to her, smiling inside that he'd entered his own essay through email. The handle he'd used wouldn't give him away, he didn't think. He reached down and helped Lilly get out of the wagon before she fell out through her own efforts.

Finn reached for her hand to steady her. Lilly waved it away. "No!"

"Sorry. Not sure where she heard that word." He grinned as Lilly's feet barely touched the floor before she started running toward the other kids who'd come to story time. He hurried over and redirected her toward the snack table with cookies arranged on pretty platters. Finn had stayed with them. "I don't want to spoil your day. But our court date's a week from Wednesday and the attorney requested you be there."

He thought some of the color drained from her face. She closed her fist and put her knuckles in her mouth pretending to bite down and then removed it. "Just kidding, trying to lighten up instead of worrying. You'll do fine. I'll be glad when it's over, for your sake."

Clint pouted. "But what about us? You and me?"

She laughed but Clint thought her heart wasn't in it. "For our next act, we'll send out fake wedding invitations."

Lilly toddled toward the dessert table and Jessica ran interference by pointing her toward a table with an Easter tree.

He loved how everything was an adventure with Finn. "Surely I'll find a brother to be our officiant. We'll start make our personalized wedding vows."

A moment of sadness flitted across her eyes and then was gone. "I've always wanted to have Mickey marry me at Disneyland! But I'll save that for my next engagement."

Her remark zinged him and he winced before he could stop himself.

But lingering longer wasn't an option, since he made a dive for Lilly, who ran away from him and grabbed a baby carrot. Twisting his body in a shape he might need medical attention for later, he sneaked along and managed to pry the vegetable from Lilly's sweet fingers before she ran somewhere else.

Finn sidled up to him, seemingly unaware he'd performed a life-saving feat, based on the carefree smile she flashed his way. She fluffed a strand of hair and gazed up at him. "Is that your human pretzel move? It's impressive."

"Her pediatrician warns me at every visit how carrots could get stuck in a kid's throat and shut off their windpipe."

She did an exaggerated frown. "Parenthood sounds like a barrel of laughs." Heading toward the area where she'd placed a chair to read, she said, "Wish me luck."

The children flocked around her, and after she sat in the chair, they plopped down on a huge rug positioned in a half circle around her chair.

"Once upon a time..." Her voice, smooth and inviting, reeled them in.

She did him, anyway.

After about twenty minutes, Finn closed the last book. The story time went better than Clint expected, although there were some bumps along the way. Lilly pulled a little boy's hair but stopped when Daddy intervened. One child dismantled an entire book-shelf of children's books while his mommy looked on. Every time Clint glanced at Finn while she read, in a romper somewhat similar to what Lilly had on, he wanted to pull her over behind the tall book cart on wheels and kiss her.

What was wrong with him? He needed her to be in the court-room, with no distractions for either of them.

She stopped the reading about the time the kids lost interest, when half her audience had wondered off. Everyone had refresh-ments, and there was a delicate plate dropped and broken, and a drink spilled, and that was by an adult.

"Well done," he said when a small cluster of customers had finished chatting with her. "You read just the right amount of time. Everything's pretty and the food's delicious."

She rested her hand on his arm and beamed up into his face. "You think so? The best thing is the moms told me how to make it better. No more glass plates." She shrugged. "Who knew?"

This felt like flirting, and he was here for it, if only it could be true. "Well, I've arranged for you to do more research. I told Sierra we'd be happy to watch Max tomorrow tonight, for her 'date night' with Wyatt."

"We?"

Willing to take a risk, he went in deeper on the thought. "We're a unit, remember?"

She covered her mouth with her hand and her eyes became small saucers, which endeared her to him even more. "See you later then, when I'll be one frightened fake fiancée. Try saying that three times. Gotta work in alliteration where I can," she teased.

Finn moved away from him to a group of women waiting for her, and Clint headed toward Jessica, with Lilly whose eyes drooped like she needed another nap.

He couldn't wait to see what tomorrow night would bring.

Chapter Eleven

F inn stood on Clint's porch with a knot in her stomach the size of her copy of *The Lord of the Rings* in one volume. She didn't think she could be more nervous if she tried. Some of her college friends had been teen babysitters. She never had.

She'd hoped yesterday to maybe see Kayla and her kids at story time. Maybe she didn't have what it took if her future sister-in-law turned her down. When Kayla called to apologize for missing story time, she said Drew had fallen on the playground and needed five stitches. Finn had offered her understanding and encouragement.

She'd always believed being prepared was the key to everything. Her right shoulder sagged with the weight of the bag she'd packed full of whatever she could possibly need for her first experience with babysitting.

She wouldn't be doing this alone. But as any woman knew, with men there was always going to be a time when you were solo. Who knew if March Madness was on tonight, or a NASCAR race or a hockey game? And then Brandon had been one who went out and played cards with the boys. She shored up her courage and rang Clint's doorbell.

The pitter patter of little feet was the only sound she heard.

She did deep breathing while she waited. How hard could this be? These kids were young and cute.

When she walked in, Clint must have sensed her tension. He took the bag from her and gave her a partial shoulder massage. In his T-shirt that said Real Men Dance, she couldn't resist patting his taut stomach.

"You're so strong. A great set of abs shouldn't be underrated."

He gave her a peck on the cheek. She'd hoped for something more but maybe not in front of the kids.

"I'm not sure what to say. I'm feeling anything but, over this lawyer thing. Lilly and Max, say hi to Finn."

"Hi," Lilly said, her voice chirpy. Max waved, a short jerky motion full of energy.

"It's good to see you two. I hope we have fun tonight."

"Hi," Lilly said.

Each turned their head, looked at each other, and ran from the room.

Without skipping a beat, Clint went right on. "Now, we're going through things slowly, step by step. Think of it like learning to ride a bicycle. You start with training wheels. That's where we are."

Finn let out a breath. She wasn't good with taking instruction and didn't want to go in that direction.

But how could Clint know that?

"You better be joking. What've you done with my bag? I brought things for the kids."

"I am kidding, but didn't know if you wanted something more formal. I've read many parenting books. Just love them and they'll love you back. It's like so many things in life. You make it up as you go, and it turns out wonderfully."

"That's a pretty great attitude. I wish you'd had a better childhood. But it seems like you've landed in a good place, and I appreciate your optimism."

He nodded, then went into another room and came back with her bag. Lilly and Max trailed him.

She went to the leather sofa that had lots of loose pillows. "You have a lovely home. It's so comfortable."

"Thanks. Home is wherever Lilly-Bear and I are, I'm finding. But I want to give her the softest landing possible, so I did a little redecorating when she came."

After propping one pillow up behind her as Finn sat down, she pulled out two books, then patted the place beside her. Max took one step forward and Lilly put her thumb in her mouth and toddled forward, too.

Clint sat down on her other side and draped his arm around her shoulders. "I love books and reading." She snuggled in by his side as the kids walked up to the sofa and squirmed their way up to sit in between her and Clint.

She handed Max's book to him. She'd chosen it, remembering she'd overheard Clint's sisters-in-law at the birthday party saying Max loved all things construction. "Here's a book about a building site. I thought you might like bulldozers."

"And dump trucks! Yellow's my favorite color." He didn't say every word perfectly but seemed good for his age. He handed his book to Clint and they started going through the pages.

Finn couldn't be more pleased that the equipment in Max's book was yellow. "Here's yours, Lilly. It's about ladybugs."

"Bu!" She took the book and turned it over in her cute little hands.

What big blue eyes Lilly had. Finn could almost see the wheels turning in her head, assessing the situation. Lilly climbed right up on her lap. She didn't weigh much, and her skin was so soft as they held the book together. Finn naturally cuddled her and smelled her mild shampoo scent.

Finn read some pages, and the little girl stopped her to point out things. Sometimes, she turned the page before Finn could read a word. She just went with the flow. Finn couldn't remember when she'd enjoyed reading so much.

Their attention spans were longer than she expected. When they lost interest, Clint said it was snack time.

"This was so much nicer than sitting in front of a room full of children. I enjoy that, too. But snuggling with you while we read is the best. Thank you for reading with me."

Max and Lilly both smiled at her, pleased with themselves for cooperating, from what she could tell.

"Oh, and you can keep the books." She opened each of their books and showed them where she had written, "To Lilly, From Finn" and "To Max, From Finn." Their eyes widened and she could see how their excitement could transfer practically by osmosis.

Clint had watched everything without comment. "Kids, what do you say to Finn?"

They both said thank you. They sounded a little like they weren't fully comfortable with English, Lilly especially. Finn spontaneously hugged them both.

Maybe she'd get the hang of this after all?

Clint fixed them finger foods and Finn mainly stood back and observed how well organized he was. Just as they finished their last bites, the doorbell rang.

"This is early for Sierra?" Clint left the room.

A few seconds later, Sierra stepped into the room with him. "Well, how'd they do?"

"Mommy!" Max called out to Sierra like she was the most important person in the world. And she probably was, to him.

Finn waited to see what Lilly would do. She'd been imitating everything Max did all evening. She had a slight crease in her forehead like she was thinking. Then she picked up her spoon and smacked it on her highchair and the moment passed.

"Thank you for letting Max visit, even though we decided to make an early evening of it." Sierra left with Max, after a goodbye that involved lots of hugging between the little ones and hugs for the adults, too. Finn stayed standing after they'd all walked to the door to say goodbye. "I think I'll head home, too."

"Stay. I mean, if you want to. I'll put Lilly to bed. It's only seven o'clock."

It seemed so much later. A lot had gone on since she'd gotten there. "Oh, I'm a night owl. I can stay out till at least eight."

"I suppose you'll turn into a pumpkin at some point. Isn't that the fate of all children's book sellers?"

"Sounds fun, but you'll have to ask someone else. I've always been more of a specialized bookstore in romance. I'm very new to offering children's books."

"I'd like to hear more about what went into that shift. Let me go and put Lilly to bed first, if that's okay."

"I'd like that. Part of the reason I was going to leave when Sierra and Max did was so I wouldn't intrude on your routine."

"You would be welcome. Routines are flexible around here. I'm just wanting to keep things as simple as possible tonight. We'll be right back."

Lilly laid her head on Clint's shoulder. "Go nigh, nigh."

"Good night, Lilly." They left the room.

Finn hadn't counted on his tenderness toward his daughter upping the attraction quotient, but it did. A big hunky man taking care of a small child, something she couldn't remember from her own childhood and hadn't seen before, was doing her in.

It made the most sense for him to put Lilly to bed alone and Finn was pleased with how she and Lilly had gotten to know one another tonight. She wanted to go slowly. While Clint went through his bedtime routine with Lilly, Finn returned a couple of emails. Then she wandered into the kitchen and ended up wiping down Lilly's highchair. She worked her way around the kitchen helping how she could, not getting into cabinets.

She reached the end of what she could do when Clint entered the kitchen. "Just what I planned, to leave the room and have you clean for me."

"You're too neat for that to have worked. I was just stretching my legs mainly."

"Could I offer you some snacks? What sounds good? I'm afraid I'm not set up well for grown-up socializing."

"I don't need food."

He busted a move, if a sway of the hips and a raised arm counted. "What's need got ta' do with it?"

"A fellow Tina Turner fan, huh? Jessica's grandma was a huge fan, when I lived with her for a time. I *thought* your dance shirt must mean something."

"Not much. Let's just say I know my way around a dance floor. Does a cup of cocoa and maybe a little cheese and crackers sound good?

"It does, actually. I meant to ask you if I'd see Cam. He lives here too, doesn't he? I hope I haven't put him out. I meant to bring this up way before now."

"This building has privacy entrances and basically a separate apartment, so we have lots of options. You're fine."

"That's really great. Jessica and I have separate apartments upstairs and it's nice to be close, you have our own spaces." If she ended up needing to share why she dropped the focus on romance books, she might need something to nibble on. They hadn't spent much time alone. The majority of their interactions had been in public, making their relationship look like they were closer than they really were.

Observing him as he went to the kitchen cabinet and found mugs and then boiled water in the microwave, Finn just felt something in the air that needed to be resolved.

She cleared her throat, a bit nervous. "Sometimes I wish we could start over and get to know each other like most people do. In some ways, it feels like we know one another well. Only we've skipped some steps because of the custody case."

He poured the water in with the hot chocolate mix and stirred it before walking over to hand hers over. She leaned with her back against the counter and he stood in front of her. "That's what I've been thinking. I know some thing about you. Your warm smile's drawn me in from the beginning. Your sharp sense of humor? Let's say I like how you keep me on my toes." He sipped from his mug and Finn tried not to fixate on his mouth as he went on. Every one of his features attracted her, separately and altogether.

"But we skimmed over the getting-to-know you stage. I know something about your rough time in high school and very little about your current business."

She sipped, then inhaled and tried to relax, staring into the hot chocolate, her stomach tense like it was their first date. When she looked up into his eyes, they were so close she noticed the yellow flecks among the blue for the first time. "Let's go back to the part about you liking my smile." She giggled, nervous all-of-a-sudden. "I'm feeling kind of uncomfortable because, where do we go from here? If anywhere?"

"I'm so glad you said something. How about we go to the couch? Baby steps. Let's take our mugs and the cheese and crackers."

She carried her mug, and it didn't take long for him to gather everything else. The small journey into the living room, she could handle. "I had a deep conversation with Kayla before you came into the book shop, and she's pretty blunt so maybe that rubbed off."

"I'm glad you did. I think she's amazing and am enjoying seeing her blossom. But we were talking about us, a subject I like better. Full disclosure? I spent a fair part of the day figuring out what to serve for snacks tonight."

She felt her cheeks heat. "You did?" The warmth of her mug seeped into her palm and relaxed her. She sat on the couch and Clint sat next to her, sharing the same large cushion.

He placed the cheese and crackers on the big wooden chest that served as a coffee table in front of them. "I looked into caviar. But not everybody likes it. Shrimp cocktail sounded good."

"I can't believe you did that."

"I wanted this to be special, our first date, sort of. Those foods used to be regulars for me. Then I switched to applesauce." He paused and she nodded to encourage him to continue. "But I didn't think we needed any more pressure, nothing more formal. Being cozy felt right, closer somehow. The cheese sticks were in the fridge, and we'll cut them with a knife and pretend it's the fancy stuff. Maybe next time..."

He was thinking about a next time? Warmth filled her. "What we're having is just fine with me. It's perfect."

"One day I'll take you to my favorite restaurant in Nashville where caviar and shrimp cocktails are on the menu. We've got an airstrip at the back of Galloway Sons Farm and a jet."

Breathe, Finn.

If he knew she was struggling for air, he didn't let on. "Now, tell me why you're new to selling children's books. What kinds of books did you sell before that?"

"Romance books, and I still do sell them. Mostly the ones that it's okay for your grandma to read. I'm branching out into children's though." She sipped the cocoa, and it went down easily. "This next part isn't something I really want to share."

He unwrapped a cheese stick and lined it up next to others on a tray. "What we feel reluctant to share usually helps the most, right You don't seem like someone who'd make a change in their business without a good reason. So why'd you do it?"

She let out a sigh. "I was broken hearted after I realized the man I'd been in a long-term relationship with didn't want what I wanted. In fact, I don't think he wanted to get married, or have kids, either. He'd gone along with my conversations about it, though. I'd sort of been imagining him in the place of the male leads in the romance stories I read. I can't do that anymore."

Clint studied her, his expression unreadable. He picked up a cracker and sliced off a piece of a cheese stick to go with it. "From a business standpoint, which books are selling more, children's or romance?"

"The romance books. Every time."

He held the cracker and cheese up to her mouth. "May I?"

She opened up and he fed the snack to her. Her lips brushing his fingers felt more intimate than their kisses somehow. Finn chewed and tried to hold it together and not choke because of how real tonight seemed. Being this close to him felt like coming home, more than anyone ever had.

After several moments, Clint gazed into her eyes. "Maybe one day you'll believe in love again, because that's what you're really saying. You don't think you can fall in love and have it work out and nobody else can either."

After downing his own cracker and a piece of cheese, Clint reached over the back of the couch, dragging down a forest green throw. He draped the soft fabric over their laps and stretched out his legs on the chest, using it for a footstool.

He scooted over and angled it so her legs, so much shorter than his, would reach the chest. "This snacks and hot chocolate idea was a good one, don't you think?"

She smiled up at him, while both of them continued to rest their feet. "I agree one hundred percent."

Then he fed her another bite, ate one himself, and they fell into a comfortable silence. After a while, he turned to her. "I want you to know our conversation the other night has stayed with me, when you talked about your daughter."

"You're really sweet. What you said about what you've been through's been on my mind, too."

"If you want to talk about your daughter, if I can help, I'm here to listen."

It seemed important to fill in this particular gap in what they knew about one another, although she wasn't sure why. "I was an only child and my dad left us when I was two. My mom was devastated and struggled to provide. When I went to prom with a basically a stranger, who wouldn't take no." She swallowed. "I told Mom I was pregnant and she told me, more or less screamed at me, that being a single mother was hard at any age and near impossible at age 17. It'd be best to opt for a closed adoption. Just put the whole experience behind me."

Clint studied her hands, and she realized she was squeezing the life out of the throw over her legs. "Look, it's my fault, for not fighting harder, for taking the easy way. I've always done what other people wanted. Jessica calls me a people pleaser sometimes. With everybody but her."

She giggled but the look in his eyes told her he wasn't amused.

Clint brought her closer, his blue eyes shiny with what could be unshed tears. "I'm so sorry. You're amazing, you know that? The way you pushed through your loss, all that you've achieved, and how you've opened your heart and helped my little girl."

His words were like a balm to her spirit, and she found herself crying, although she didn't lose control. *Thank you, Lord.*

Clint pulled a tissue from a box on the side table, handed it to her, and she dabbed her eyes.

"If you don't mind my asking, how did you end up divorced when you seem like a family man?"

"With me coming from foster care, and Trixie's parents with multiple divorces, we didn't have a chance. She ran around on me from the start. After one of our trial separations, we agreed to try one more time. That's when she became pregnant with Lilly." He paused, stood, and paced around the room. "It's important to me that you understand I didn't abandon my daughter. Trixie refused to change after Lilly was born. She filed for divorce." He ran his fingers through his hair. "I blame myself for giving up too easily."

Finn stood and went to him. She took his hands in hers. "You did all you could. I know because look how hard you're working now."

Clint stared at the pile of wrappings and empty mugs on the table. "I'm glad Trixie and I married because we had Lilly."

"All of that sounds hard on everybody. Lilly's had a tough time."

He put everything on the tray. "That's why I'm knocking myself out to make it up to her. Oh, and I'm socking away money for her therapy," he said. Then he laughed. "Hard as I try, I mess up every day. But, enough about me. Tell me what else about your bookstore. Your enthusiasm for your work inspires me. I'm in the preliminary stages of breeding horses at the farm. My new-found brothers are backing me and partnering with me, too."

Clint picked up the tray and she followed him into the kitchen where he pulled out a drawer with a trash bin inside, then tossed in the cheese wrappers.

She took the mugs off the tray and set them in the sink. "That's wonderful news. Sounds like God isn't done with either of us, and forgiving ourselves is our first battle. It's hard keeping my bookstore going and it's too important to let go. In elementary school, I didn't fit in, as a lonely child, one who didn't have the house with the white picket fence. Losing myself in books, and having librarians who befriended me, that's what saved me. When I found out how many expensive degrees librarians need, I cried for days. I couldn't see how I'd ever have my dream of becoming a librarian. A bookstore is a close second. My life changed in 5th grade, we moved here, and Jessica became friends with me."

"And the rest is history?" Clint pulled a glass out of the cabinet and walked toward a refrigerator that must have been as big as her first apartment. "We've been talking for a while. Would you like some water?"

At her nod, he used the icemaker and when he handed her the glass, she took a long drink. "Sorry if I'm ranting, because it seemed more than venting. I know I'm too, too…" She swirled her hand in the air. "Something."

"Not to me, you're not."

He came over, so close she fell into the blue depths of his eyes. Finn wanted Clint to kiss her. He leaned in and pressed his lips to hers. She reached up, ran her fingers through the hair at the nape of his neck and kissed him back. His lips hinted of chocolate, and were firm yet tender, healing even. She didn't want it to end.

Finally, he pulled away and she clung for a moment longer while he said, "I've wanted to do that all evening."

"Look, I've had a nice evening. Getting to know your family's been so enjoyable. Seeing how Max greeted his mommy was really sweet. I appreciate seeing how others live."

They stood at the sink and Clint soaped the mugs and she

rinsed. "Finn, I hate to break this to you, because I'm thinking you might want other people's lives to fall into place like yours didn't. Everyone's life has rough places. Maybe realizing that will help you see the beauty in yours. See, Sierra adopted Max. She's not his biological mother. They're a beautiful, blended family and he's Wyatt's son. His mother died and Sierra adopted him when she married Wyatt."

Finn shrugged. "Maybe the toughest places in our lives help us to appreciate the beautiful ones. You think?"

Finn went out of the kitchen and slumped back onto the couch cushion. Lots of people didn't have the so-called ideal family. Unless she got to know them like she did the Galloways, she would never know. It was a testament to Wyatt and Sierra that Max was so happy and seemed well-adjusted, although, who ever really knew?

Clint wandered into the room and studied her, his mouth in a solid line, thinking deeply, it seemed. "Do you mind if I ask you something?"

"Go ahead but no guarantees I'll answer you."

He threw his head back and laughed. But it wasn't the same without his cowboy hat. "If there was a way to find Emily, would you want to? Because my lawyer said he'd help."

What a question. Her heartbeat kicked up just thinking about it. She'd thought about her daughter every day of her life since giving birth.

"You don't make it easy, do you? I mean, first you ask me to marry you when we've never met before. Now you're offering to help me meet my daughter again. I've wished I could since the moment I let her go, but that could disrupt her life. Maybe mine, too." She stood up ran her fingers through her hair. "I'm assuming you're asking for a reason?"

"The attorney sent me papers for you to sign, if you want his help."

Her heart was beating so loud in her ears he could surely hear it. "Sounds expensive."

"You're not answering my question. Just think about it, okay?"

She dragged out her half empty water bottle and took a drink. "I've thought about it. My answer is yes."

He walked over to a long piece of furniture they would have called a credenza in the offices that were near her former bookstore. Her ex worked in one of the offices. Jessica and been there and said to call the furniture a console now.

Clint pulled out some papers. "Now just sign where those little sticky notes say to. That'll get the process started."

She was so nervous she used her left hand to steady the right one.

Finn finished and he took the papers to put them away. "I'll hand deliver them at my appointment with the lawyer."

She reached for them and he let her have the papers back. "I'd be more comfortable taking them to the lawyer myself. I'll tack a note to it with any details I can think of that might help. Thank you so much."

Finn found her bag and tucked the papers inside.

When she returned, Clint's intense look made her heart race, as he seemed to have something to say. "You know, I've found it difficult to be fake the way we are and not move into real, to hold back for Lilly's custody hearing. Parameters can be good though."

Not if you thought about going past them as much as she was starting to.

"I'd like to light this. Will that bother your allergies?"

Until now, she hadn't noticed the candle in his hand. It pleased her, somehow, that he remembered a small thing about her, like how a dog in the bakery had made her sneeze the day they met.

"I don't think so. Give it a try."

He went right to where the lighter was, and the flame appeared almost immediately. "Let's dance."

She nodded. She didn't want to turn him down. "Any chance you've got enough dance chops for both of us?"

Clint slipped his arm around her waist and they went together as he put a vinyl record on his turntable. Slow music from another era filled the room. Clint's arms surrounded her. The scent of his aftershave had been with her all evening and the closeness of being in his arms took over. She didn't think of anything but them, together like they seemed destined to be.

Oh no, some types of music would get her thinking this way. As soon as *Begin the Beguine* played, that her mother used to sing, Finn knew she was a goner.

One record would end, all romance and rhythm, and Clint would go put on another one. She felt every muscle relax as they danced. What they were doing was more like swaying to the music.

Finally, he went to change an album, and she came out of her trance to see the time on her watch. She put her hand on Clint's arm. "It's almost midnight. Time for me to go home. My pumpkin tendrils might start to sprout."

The corners of his mouth twitched up. "I thought maybe if the music didn't stop, you wouldn't go. This has been the most fun I've had in ages."

"Clearly, you don't get out enough. Even when I came a little unglued talking?"

"Especially that part."

She giggled. "Well good, because there's more where that came from."

"You don't have to threaten me."

He took a few steps to a coat rack where he'd hung her jacket earlier. His shoulders were shaking, and she realized he was laughing.

"I've laughed so much since meeting you. After tonight, I feel like I know you better. I want to know everything about you, Finn."

He bundled her coat up around her and buttoned it.

She unbuttoned the top two buttons and inhaled air. "It's almost 50 degrees out."

He shrugged. "Sorry. Guess I'm feeling protective after what you shared tonight. Seventeen's a baby, to me."

He leaned in and kissed her, his mouth tender yet firm, familiar already. He wrapped his arms around her, and she rested on him as they extended the kiss. He released her, and she'd never felt so treasured.

His voice gruff, he murmured, "If we don't stop it'll be Saturday morning. The full Galloway crew's meeting for breakfast. They'll know I was up very late because they say I look different when I'm sleep-deprived."

"You could've just shoved me out the door instead of making that silly excuse. I'll leave now to protect your reputation."

His expression turned serious, and she might've detected sadness. Was it something she'd done? They'd had such a good time.

"I think it'd be best if we don't see so much of each other. This is feeling all too real."

She frowned. She'd just let her guard down and now this? "I promise not to dump anymore rants on you."

He gave a half-hearted smile. "I'm getting fond of you and I need to concentrate to prepare for court."

It took self-control not to stomp her foot. "I don't believe you. There has to be more reason than that."

"Since it's not working out to come in during the week and do the repairs when you have customers, I wouldn't be coming in much anyway and it'll be easier this way. We know we're sort of taking a week off."

"I'd appreciate it if you'd let me know if there's more to it."

"Not that I'm aware of, there isn't. I have to get the character part of the court date together. It's a lot. I need time to sort things out. I'll be there helping when we all come together to help with your repairs a week from tomorrow, okay?"

She pulled the door forward to leave and made it out to her car, just barely, before the tears came.

It wasn't a gusher, though. A week wasn't forever. She'd had too good a time to think anything was seriously wrong. On her way home, Finn reminded herself their fake relationship would be coming to an end soon anyway. Then why had it felt as though it was just getting started? Her mind reeled, wondering if she'd done something to cause Clint to withdraw. Questioning if she'd meet Emily one day, finally.

When she pulled up to her parking space, Jessica was upstairs on her balcony. Finn shut off the car, scrambled out, and hurried inside. She hadn't realized how much she wanted some company after her full night.

Jessica met her on the stairs. "You okay?"

That was all it took for the dam to break. Tears flooded her cheeks. When her best friend led her up the stairs into Jessica's own apartment, Finn sunk down on the couch. The huge piece of old furniture was covered with a sheet, ready for her to sleep over.

There was a lull in her emotional meltdown.

"Finn, I'm sure you're exhausted. I was starting to think you weren't coming home tonight."

Thinking of Clint pulling back after how they'd spent their night turned her waterworks back on. "I don't want to talk about it." She sobbed between words.

"We'll talk later, if you want to. It's okay to wake me up even." Jessica hugged her, then went into her bedroom. Finn puttered around getting ready for bed, keeping a tissue handy. They both kept spares of all the products they needed for each other.

Finally, Finn lay on the couch, her nose stuffed up so badly she couldn't breathe. At last, the questions she had no answers for exhausted her to the point that she fell into a deep sleep.

Chapter Twelve

Clint couldn't remember when a week had felt so long as he waited outside Wind in the Willows for Finn to get there and let him in. The local crowd came out on Saturday and Main Street had cars parked all along the curbs. A mom and dad went in with two little kids to Delaney's. He and his brothers sometimes went there on Saturdays for the special kids' breakfast menu.

What would it be like to go somewhere as a family of his own, to have someone to laugh with? He'd kind of had that with Finn in small pieces. But she'd be moving on soon. An ache sort of happened near his heart when he thought of losing her. Lilly liked her, too.

He checked his phone clock. She'd texted him two minutes ago that she was running a little late. For some reason he couldn't explain, he wanted to see her right now. He put his toolbox on the porch and walked back to his truck to bring in more of what they would need.

He hadn't really stayed true to staying away for a week. Or at least he tried not to.

Mid-week he had planned to take Lilly to story time and had been counting the days for that, if he was being honest. He was going to surprise Finn. Then she'd caught a cold and cancelled story time. Jessica had called and let him know, which seemed strange. He was on a list for group text messages for when the schedule changed.

He'd offered to bring her chicken soup, but Jessica relayed the message to him that Finn said she wasn't that sick. She hadn't wanted to take a chance on spreading her germs to him and Lilly, either.

"Hey, I'm sorry I'm late." Finn had come up behind him and she slid her hand into the crook of his elbow.

It made him feel good, that maybe they'd pick up where they left off, at some point. "Don't you park in the back?"

"Usually. But I thought you and your brothers might need to carry in something big."

They walked side by side as he carried his things. "It's so good to see you. Feeling all better? Seems like it's been forever."

Finn unlocked the door, and they passed the plants on their way inside. "I am. It wasn't great but I turned the corner pretty quickly. I don't think I'm contagious, if that's why you're asking."

"I don't want you to be sick, of course. But I also want to be well myself, for the court date. I didn't think you'd expose me to anything but wanted to double check."

Clint made two trips to bring his tools and cloths in, determined not to let her know how he felt. It might scare her off, that he had feelings for her. He couldn't take his eye off the goal now, which was to show a unified front to the judge.

With his tools all inside on the floor, he looked over at Finn. She sat at a decorative table with a glass top barely big enough for one person, let alone two. Looking for an alternative seat, for the first time he took in the pastel bows tacked up on the corners of the food cases, and a decal of an old-fashioned Mr. and Mrs. Bunny with a basket had been added to the front window.

He pulled out the seat across from her and sat down. "This place is a bit cutesy. You call this a table? I'm in danger of losing my man card in here."

Placing her elbows on the table and putting her chin in her

hands, Finn beamed. "If you ever did, you'd get it back real quick with that cowboy hat alone."

Something warmed inside of him, and he leaned back, away from her fruity scent and those eyes that called to him.

Whoa, boy. He'd better get down to business. "There's all kinds of catching up we could do, if you wanted to that is. But since we're meeting early before the rest to go over the plan . . ."

The bell above the door jingled and Jessica hurried into the shop, her arms full of baking things like pans and potholders. "Sorry, the store was a zoo. You'd think it was Easter already. Hope I haven't missed anything."

Finn jumped up, and her face turned pink. "Nope. Let me help you." She started pulling plates, muffin cups with bunnies on them, and other things from Jessica and putting them on the counter.

Jessica strode to the back and returned carrying a tall stool, which she dragged over beside their table and perched on. "So, how's the court date prep going? Won't be long now."

Finn sat back down and Clint didn't have the energy to make things up. With her so close, resisting taking her into his arms was all he could muster. "I'm very on edge about the court date. I wanted to stay away from Finn and make sure nothing went wrong." Which included making sure he didn't kiss Finn some more or cross any boundaries.

"But honestly, I went a little nuts watching tips online about 'how to make your court date go well.' They talked about keeping your normal routines because kids can tell when you're upset, and sometimes what you think might help could backfire, depending on the judge. There were tons of videos of kids getting their arms broken or chopping their hair all off, and judges giving the other parent custody. I've pretty much wrapped Lilly in bubble pack until this is over."

"We all wish you the best," Jessica said.

"She helped me get the perfect court dress," Finn said. "I was online, too, thinking about the court date. Dress shopping, doing my part."

It was nice to have support but now he needed to get into what he came for. He was looking forward to having something else occupy his mind.

He got on his pad to run through a slide presentation. "This'll help you get to know the work we're doing and us, too. We know we're sort of unique with so many brothers. But we're all distinctly different and each bring something to the table."

Jessica got out a little notepad from her pocket. Clint's chest tightened. He'd put this together on the fly while he rocked Lilly. She was teething.

"I know you've volunteered and didn't have to do this presentation," Jessica said. "I feel bad I don't have any food to offer you, but The Sweet Shop's closed today so you can work here and there's going to be dust everywhere so I wouldn't want to have the health department surprise me or anything. I can offer you a bottled water."

Admitting his mouth had been watering for one of her cinnamon rolls might reveal his weakness. He simply fiddled with his tablet. "Oh, I don't need anything. Since my family offered what we can to the community after the tornado, we developed an informal presentation. Mainly, donating our services shouldn't make you feel you can't ask questions, and we want you to tell us if you think something doesn't look right."

A picture of Caleb appeared on the screen. Since people tended to mix them up, they thought a photos and short biographies at the beginning might help.

Jessica jotted down notes in her notebook. "Since I inherited the building, I'll have the final say about what is done. Preserving its history is important to me."

Slides explained Caleb owned a construction firm he had run himself before moving to Fair Creek. The brothers had photos of their families. Clint read some bullet points explainingCaleb had analyzed what was needed to fix the crumbling bricks. He determined some were too broken and couldn't be salvaged. So when Leo was introduced, Finn explained how Leo'd used his artist's eye to be sure the new bricks matched as much as possible. He'd researched how to restore the mortar between the bricks so it looked the most appealing, too.

Finn paid close attention, and it made Clint feel like she was really interested. The spindly-legged table they'd chosen to sit at barely held Clint's laptop. If he shifted, he might lose his computer or fall from his seat. Also, he was practically sitting on top of Finn. Their knees touched, and he shifted. The scent of her shampoo wafted over and made it a hard to concentrate. He wanted what they'd had and it was torturous to be so close, yet feel so far apart.

Though their engagement was fake, he felt responsible for anything associated with Finn. So when he finished with the slides, he spoke to the women directly.

"As you can see, my brothers and I definitely all have different personalities. Given a choice, I would never put them in one room together, especially if they were surrounded by hand saws, hammers, nails and anything else heavy that is associated with a hardware store."

They smiled at each other and gave him a nod.

The front door opened, and the bell jingled. Leo came in the store. "What'er you guys doin' sitting around? Talking is way overrated, too, when it's time to get the work done. We don't have room for any slackers here."

Jessica stood and spoke so everyone could hear. Clint's given us an excellent presentation on what we can expect today. I've had other people present to me that were high-priced and yours would stand up against those."

Finn had just found a stool to lean on so she could retie her shoe. One shoe was still untied but she stood. "I'm ready to work. I mean, I don't know anything about bricks. But, show me what to do."

There was a tap on the door. Caleb and Wyatt came in

carrying a tall ladder between them. Caleb spoke first. "Yeah, I'm glad to hear you're a good worker, Finn. I heard you were caught talking with our brother Clint when you were supposed to be working. It's not like you two have anything to talk about that's more important than work. Not like you're engaged or anything."

Clint was pretty sure his brothers were teasing Finn. Clint said. "Thanks for understanding, guys. Being engaged is pretty much a full-time job so I hope it's okay if we don't stay long."

Wyatt started fixing to set up the legs of the ladder. "You better talk now, you two, 'cause once you get married, the communication level really drops off. Just sayin'."

Finn's forehead had a wrinkle only Clint knew about and it indicated she was concentrating. "No, we're not doing anything about our engagement. Maybe there's something we should be doing but we're not. I'll be staying to help."

Finn looked from one brother to the other as they continued on their tasks, like she was trying to remember their names. "You all are a well-oiled machine!"

After almost four hours, a part of the worst wall had been repaired. Another less major issue was finished, and they'd found and repaired a leak Jessica hadn't known was there.

The door jingled and Cam walked in.

"Nice you could make it." Leo was the oldest, except for Clint and his twin but they'd come late to the family. He could say what others couldn't.

If there were a way to mentally send a message to Cam, Clint would have.

"Thanks for giving me the benefit of the doubt." Sarcasm dripped from Cam. "I had a mechanical breakdown at the far end of the property. Nobody could fix it. Thought about not comin' at all and this is the attitude—"

Wyatt interrupted Cam. "You're going to have to learn sometimes it's better not to show up, if you're not going to help anything."

"Why do I feel like you're referring to the town meeting I

showed up to about your solar energy? Just come out and say it. Just like I have a right to be here now even though I'm late, I had a right to give my opinion at that meeting!" Cam's voice filled the space.

Wyatt's face was a pinkish color, on its way to red, Clint figured. "You sure did! You gave your opinion when it was damaging to this family!" Wyatt's words were like the sounds of shotguns firing. The tension in their shoulders and their stances said they wanted a reason to start punching.

Caleb set his tools for his brick work aside and no one else appeared to be on task, either. Most were watching what was going on, and Jessica frowned as she pulled Finn back and placed her arm loosely around her shoulder. It was Finn that worried Clint most. He didn't know how she'd take this, not being used to family dynamics, or fireworks, either.

Clint thought back to when he and Finn exchanged their information to learn more about one another. She'd said she was an only child. She might not know how siblings worked, especially brothers. His brothers could be rough when it came to teasing. They were impossible to deal with when they felt wronged. In this case both men had the feeling, he believed.

Leo came to the center of the room. "We're not gonna be able to settle this today. We're done here. When you two cool down, I'd like to meet with you and talk things over. Maybe you'll air your differences, and I'll knock some sense into you, if I have to. What do you say?"

Clint couldn't tell anything by Wyatt's body language, but he sensed Cam was ready to try for a truce. His fists were relaxed and down at his side. His face wasn't red anymore. Finally, Wyatt spoke. "I'd welcome the chance to meet about this, get things settled."

Cam nodded his agreement.

"Okay then! Good work today. Got a lot done in a short time. Now we're off to hide Easter eggs. Meet at the farm ASAP."

The drop cloths, mortar, and ladders were put away lickety-split, a word Clint had always heard but this was the first time he'd seen it in action so much. Dust rose as people shuffled out. Nobody liked conflict, especially not among the brothers.

He couldn't get to Finn fast enough. When she saw him, she didn't come to him, so he went up to her. "I reckon it's my own fault."

There was fire in her eyes, which seemed better than fear. "Whatever you're thinking of, you're probably right."

He laughed. "Will you ride out to the farm with me? The Easter egg hunt will do us all some good."

"Well, all the Easter essay contest stuff's in my SUV so I'll need to go in that."

He tipped his hat. "Well, Maam, I'd much rather drive my truck. But will you let me drive you, at least?"

i "Sure can." It meant she must trust him a little and he was good with that. "Let me get my keys. They're in my purse."

She darted off, and he liked seeing her so excited. She seemed like a genuinely nice person. He made small talk with Jessica. But he felt bad to be leaving her out, although they were going to a Galloway get-together meant for family only.

"I'm sorry I'm always taking Finn away from you. But today we're going to my family's pre-egg hunt. It's before the community one later you're welcome to come to."

Some cowboy boot steps on the partly restored floor alerted him to someone approaching. Cam had changed his shirt into something with pale plaid. He passed Clint and went up to Jessica. "Are you ready?"

She nodded. "Always ready for anything." Cam headed toward the door as Jessica grinned at Clint and gave a little wave. "See you at the Galloway pre-egg hunt."

What was that about?

Chapter Thirteen

Clint drove Finn's SUV toward Galloway Sons Farm and the vehicle was more comfortable than he expected. He put the windows down a little, so he didn't risk blowing Finn's hat off.

He glanced over at Finn in the passenger seat across from him. She had her hand on top of her hat, but she smiled. "Spring's my favorite season."

"Same here."

"I admire what you're wearing. You look like you belong in an Easter parade somewhere."

"Thank you! I don't think you've ever complimented me on my clothes before."

He thought she must be mistaken. He'd liked almost everything she'd worn, he was sure. Maybe he hadn't told her. "Well, I'm going to have to change that. I'll start by saying that's one great hat. It's perfect for you."

When she turned to him, he didn't see how her smile could be any brighter. "It was my mother's. I found a milliner. You know, I always feel that word's too stuffy. Mom didn't have much but she loved her hats. There's a hat shop that cleaned it up for me and restored it."

"I haven't been the easiest to be around and I'm not handling the upcoming trial well. But it's nice to be together. I've missed you."

Maybe it was time he acted like their relationship would last past the trial. During their week apart, he'd prayed in the quiet he'd experienced, the sleepless nights. He'd gotten the message to stop looking at her as someone only for his use. He hadn't been quite that bad, but he hadn't been good either.

He needed to believe he'd keep Lilly, too. "Easter is such a hopeful time. For some reason, getting your hat cleaned up reminds me of the real reason for Easter. We all need to be cleaned up in one way or the other."

"I've appreciated how you've listened to me, not judging my story and the events that've shaped my life."

Clint drove in silence and enjoyed the open fields and the horses, the sheep with their lambs, and the cows. They were all beautiful to him.

He didn't like the cold and had missed Tennessee during winter, but this warm weather was here to stay. "I thought the cold would never end. And now, here we are."

"I know. Can't believe it's the beginning of April. I love it when Easter comes closer to spring like this."

They were getting close to the farm. "Here's the plan. Since our family's hosting the community egg hunt, we decided to have one for ourselves. But it's a pre-hunt or really a reverse hunt."

"Let me guess. Are you letting the kids hide the eggs?"

Clint steered into the parking spots at Wyatt and Sierra's house. "We're here to pick up Lilly. You're right. It makes sense, doesn't it?"

He shut off the car, got out of his seat, and went around to Finn's door. He opened her door, and she about jumped out of her skin. "Oh, you scared me. I thought you were going in to get Lilly on your own."

"Won't you come with me? For one thing, I'll need to get Lilly's car seat. I know she's missed you. I thought I'd give her the gift of some alone time with you before we get into the crowd and excitement."

"That's one of the nicest things anyone's said to me. I'd love to get to know Lilly, at her own pace. I'm all about her taking the lead. Thank you for giving me such a warm welcome with your daughter."

He held out his hand and she slipped hers right in, and he enjoyed the soft touch of her skin as they walked the distance to the farmhouse. "This is more cars than I've seen over here in a while. Easter's something special with us. You walking okay? I don't know how you manage in this yard with those heels. Don't twist an ankle or anything."

"My secret is holding hands with a handsome cowboy every chance I get."

Inside the farmhouse some of the children were running around and others were hopping, pretending to be the Easter bunny.

Clint would've spotted Lilly anywhere. Her wavy hair had turned curly from running around with her cousins, and her skin glowed, as one of his foster grandmother's used to say. Women didn't sweat, according to her, and the memory reminded him his young life hadn't gone all wrong. There'd been some kind people who'd been hard to part with.

"Daddy!" Lilly shrieked, and he loved it. He'd have to get her to stop screaming one day, if she didn't grow out of it. For now, he was thrilled she called his name and said it so clearly. At her young age, he liked to think she understood some of the Easter message, and he always appreciated when she expressed joy, especially when she saw him.

"I...nn!" Finn's smile at hearing her name coming from Lilly's mouth, or trying to, was priceless. His sisters-in-law had fed his child right along with theirs. He was grateful he could take her straight to where they were hosting the egg hunt this year.

After a few more minutes of chaos, it was time to head out and he scooped Lilly up. Slinging her bag of baby gear over one shoulder, he grabbed her car seat, then took hold of Finn's hand as they went back to the car. He smiled inwardly that he'd learned how to manage all of this, including how to secure Lilly safely to ride in Finn's vehicle.

By the time they were pulling up to the huge field that managed to have green grass, there were packs of Galloway children already on the scene. The straight, newly grown grass was the perfect height to hide eggs. It looked like fine hair and Clint loved that farmers knew things other people sometimes couldn't. He'd heard it was grown and transplanted like sod. That could have been a rumor. Farmers were the biggest jokers, he'd learned since moving here.

The large, mechanical bunnies from Vintage Finds had been brought to the farm the night before. They were arranged all in a row like nutcrackers at Christmas.

Clint unfastened Lilly from her car seat, which had faced the seat and kept her from seeing the set-up for herself. Her eyes sparkled at seeing the children and Easter decorations. "Bunny!"

Lilly's excitement brought up his energy level. Seeing things with her made them an extra treat for him.

Finn stood by Clint and took in the spectacle. Adults were managing big boxes full of Easter baskets. Someone had rigged up a sound system through the hay mow in the barn. "Attention, please! Get in line to pick up your Easter basket. Then proceed to the egg pick-up."

"This is unbelievable. I'm glad I'm seeing it with my own eyes."

Lilly's cousin Chloe, Annie and Caleb's nine-year-old daughter came over to her."

His little girl couldn't say her name but shouted "Co."

"Lilly. Come see the baskets!"

Lilly dove into Chloe's arms. "She wants to be with you so much," Clint said. "This is Finn. We're coming along, too, okay? But you can be in charge."

She nodded and they started toward the action.

Areas had been marked off by age group. Instead of looking for eggs, the kids were going to hide them. The community children would be coming soon. The eggs couldn't be trusted to be outside overnight, not with animals all around.

The children all had baskets full of plastic eggs filled with candy, hand stuffed courtesy of the coffee group at Delaney's.

A whistle sounded to start them from where they were lined up.

It turned out to be a fast process and Clint and Finn stood with the adults. Kayla came over to them. "Ella and Drew are teaming up together today."

Finn gave Kayla a grin of approval and made the thumbs up sign. "Good for you!

"I know. It's a first. Maybe I'll have some peace at our house yet."

* * *

Finn worked on the essay project in a mini barn on the farm, unable to wipe the smile from her face as she sorted out the prizes. She loved everyone's essays and didn't want to name a winner. But what was the point of that? In the end, she'd decided on nine winners, choosing three adults, three teenagers, and three younger children.

Finn looked up and Jessica was walking toward her. "What're you doing? How'd you find me here?" She waved her arm around the tiny building.

Jessica hugged her. "You know I've got special radar when it comes to you."

"Thanks so much for being my tie-breaker judge on the essays. They were so good and the decisions weren't easy. I mean, deciding between, 'Ode to an Easter Egg,' and 'I Saw Mommy Kissing the Easter Bunny' was beyond me."

"I know, that first one cracked me up!" Jessica held her stomach while she laughed, then patted Finn's arm. "You can't worry about hurting people's feelings. I'm not saying to be mean but the point of a contest is competition. This is where our differences are an asset."

"I hadn't looked at it that way."

An announcement came over the loudspeakers. "First call for the Easter essay contest. Go to the stage under the oak tree."

Finn picked up the basket where she'd organized everything. Her heart was beating a little faster. "Would you believe I'm nervous?"

"Aw, how come? Give it to me. I'll do it for you and not be bothered. I wish you'd let me work on helping you."

"Oh, you've helped me enough. Take that how you will. I am how I am." Announcing the winners herself would be good for her. "You know growing up I didn't want to cause anybody trouble. My mom had enough to deal with. What if people are mad about who was chosen?"

"Send 'em to me. I'll explain the meaning of a competition. Besides, I thought you were giving them everybody their 15 seconds of fame by collecting them all into a book.

"It's supposed to be 15 minutes but in a small town, seconds'll have to do. I'm creating an anthology. Also, people should really respect how we did the essays, having blind judging. It's going to be interesting to find out the names of the writers."

"Second and last call for the Easter essay contest." The speaker system really did help keep things organized.

"I better get over to the place they're using for a stage. Want to come?"

Jessica shook her head. "I came with Cam Galloway. Did you know?"

Picking up her papers, Finn began putting them in her bag. "Clint told me. How's it going?"

"Oh, it's fine. We're just friends. I like him though."

"Well, it's early in the relationship. Maybe something will come of it." Since when had Finn ever given any kind of advice on men? What was happening to her?

"I don't know. It's not every day someone looks at anyone the way Clint looks at you."

Finn's stomach did a little flutter. "What's that supposed to mean? We chit-chat about nothing for days and then you spring that on me? And I'm due somewhere right now?"

Could Jessica be right? Finn swept off every tool and pen from the table into her bag, randomly leaving things where they ended up.

Jessica shrugged. "I said what I said."

Slinging her bag over her shoulder, Finn hustled toward the door and Jessica followed. This conversation was getting more strange by the minute. *Had* Clint looked at her differently and she'd been too dense to notice?

Jessica checked her watch. "I gotta go meet Cam. He's trying to get bowling together or something. Nothing cool like Clint and his photography. Don't get me wrong. I'm not interested in Clint. I just don't understand why you aren't."

They were at the place where they had to go their separate ways, which was a relief from all the confusing feelings she'd stirred. Finn waved goodbye. Jessica didn't know her innermost thoughts, because she liked Clint, a lot. She just wasn't sure how much.

Seeing all the kids with their Easter candy as she went by lightened her spirits. Pastel malted milk eggs, her favorite. Wicker baskets made of multiple colors like when she was a kid. Sometimes it was the simpler things. Was God trying to tell her something?

Could Jessica be right about how Clint felt about Finn?

There wasn't time to mull it over because Clint joined her by the dunking booth. "I've always thought it would be fun to have people try to dunk me in one of those things."

"Oh no, not me."

She seemed to be confronted on all sides about being different from other people. Maybe she could learn not to let that bother her.

Clint fell into step with her. "I'm going to your contest announcements session. I've never heard you speak in public other than reading. Hey, I've got a one-track mind, thinking about the court date. It's almost here. Do you think we'll still want to learn things about each other after that?"

It was as though Clint and Jessica had sipped some kind of potion, from the way they both quizzed her. "That's a good question. I don't have an answer for you. I've got to get through these announcements. Now that you've called it 'public speaking,' I'm not so relaxed." Good thing she'd mentally rehearsed some of what she planned to say.

Clint put his hand on her shoulder like he knew she was distracted. "I'm going to want to, to keep getting to know you. So I'll hope you'll keep that in mind."

He'd risked sharing his feelings, which took Finn's breath away, while at the same time making her realize she wasn't ready to do that. "I appreciate you're saying that. Focusing on the court case so much has made me consider 'us' as temporary. Jessica's encouraging me to think longer term." She gave his arm a light punch. "For some reason, she thinks we're good for each other. I'm just not sure whether I'm ready. It feels like a big decision, for me anyway. "

"You're fine. I just don't want to lose you because I didn't tell you how I feel."

His words were something she'd really wanted to hear after that evening she'd spent at his place. Then he'd pulled back, and although he said it was because of the unresolved custody dispute, she couldn't be sure. All she'd wanted her whole life was to be confident, though. So this was just one more thing.

"I'm not sure how I feel. I can't even tell you what would need to happen for me to know. I'll try to figure that out, because I wouldn't want to stand in your way of finding whatever you want."

His shoulders seemed to relax. "I'm good with that."

They came to the stage area. Only a few people were in the

audience, not as many as she'd hoped. Shirley and Amelia were there and waved to her.

Finn approached the stage. She thought Clint would take his seat, but he stayed right with her. Off to the side, there were rickety metal stair steps leading on to the stage.

As Finn started up, her heel caught in the grate-like material the step was made of, and she tilted forward.

"I've got you." Clint's muscled arm went around her, catching her before she fell. She looked up into his handsome face. He must have positioned himself beside the stairs, in case she needed him. He reached down and got her heel unstuck, then swept her up in his arms and set her up on stage. It all happened so quickly no one seemed to have noticed. She certainly did though.

She squatted down on stage to speak on his level. "Thank you for saving me from falling." He nodded and then turned to walk away when she said, "Clint." He looked at her. "What you just did? That's going to help me know. I haven't really had someone to catch me, not anyone I've ever dated anyway."

He smiled, then did a little jump in the air like she'd only seen in photos, and went to find his seat.

Finn didn't know the third and second place children's winners. She was glad they were there so she could recognize them and give them their certificates and gift cards from local businesses.

Looking out into the audience, Finn could guess who this next winner was, seeing the person's undercover name. "First prize goes to AmeliaBedelia."

Shirley let out a whoop and her daughter's face turned pink. Amelia tried not to show her excitement, walking at a slower pace, and not really smiling, as she made her way to the stage.

An image of herself at that age flitted through Finn's head, maybe because Amelia had lost her dad at a young age, too. The girl walked with a confidence Finn had lacked. Shirley was able to give what her daughter needed, it appeared, when Finn's Mom struggled too much just to sustain them.

Amelia made it up on stage. No one else had the heels that didn't work. "Here you go, girl." She gave Amelia her certificate and gift card. "Good job. Now here's a booklet of everyone's essays."

"Thanks! I hope you do this again sometime. It was fun."

"I probably will." Amelia hugged Finn. Then she walked off the stage.

The girl's response caught her off guard, both her asking for what she wanted and coming in for the hug. Finn had held herself in for so long, but the connections to this town, maybe even to the Galloway family, were reaching into her heart, like wrapping her in a huge, collective, hug. Maybe she could belong to someone, to something.

"Third prize in the adult category goes to a writer who used a handle. Plus, they had someone else turn it in for them, so they wouldn't be discovered. Secretly Engaged, come to the stage."

Clint stood up and headed toward her. She must be losing her edge. Of course it was Clint. She just wasn't thinking of him as a writer, and the child in the essay hadn't been named. Some of the wording was among the more tender sentiments she remembered ever reading. When he reached the stage, she announced his name. "This is Clint Galloway, everybody. His unique essay was about what his child means to him. It's really elegantly written and touched my heart."

Finn hugged Clint, and spoke into her ear, far away from the microphone. "There's a lot you don't know about me." The man knew what to say to make her heart rate kick up.

Turning toward the audience, Finn realized she was fine with competition, as long as it was fair. "Y'all know Clint and I are engaged. I really didn't know the essay was his, and we had an outside judge who made the final decisions anyway. His essay wasn't picked as a favorite by me alone, and I just wanted you to know that."

While the audience clapped, Finn presented Clint with his prize, with the essays she'd made into a booklet right on top. Clint's coloring rose a bit at seeing Lilly in the photo he'd taken. When he turned to leave, Finn hooked the the mic onto the stand to walk him to the edge of the stage. "I like what I know about you more every day. You're keeping me guessing."

The last prize of the evening was all that separated her from finishing her task. "First place goes to News Girl!" Alice, the *Gazette* newspaper publisher, stood.

As the grand prize winner moved to the front, Finn couldn't resist going into detail. "When I came up with this essay contest, I wasn't sure if anyone would even participate. We received well over twenty. Some were serious, others were sad, and a couple of you wrote poetry. Alice's entry, "Ode to an Easter Egg," offered a little of everything, with humor, a prayer of thanks to God for creating the egg, and even statistics on eggs. Last year, Indiana produced enough eggs to make it second out of all the states in the USA—10.8 billion. I'm sure a large part of those came from farmers in the Fair Creek area, so we can be proud!"

Somebody started the clapping and after it died down, Finn spoke into the mic. "You're all winners in my book. Everyone who entered gets a free copy of the anthology. Give yourselves a round of applause and let's all go home and read."

Clint helped her get down off stage, then went off to check on Lilly while Finn put together the awards paperwork and let people get the booklets.

Alice hung around and then sought Finn. "I'd like to interview you. What do you think?"

"I'll check my schedule and get back with you." A story on her wouldn't be interesting, and appearing in Alice's little newspaper wouldn't mean much.

Alice followed as she headed to the little barn.

"Most people would jump at the chance."

She couldn't be serious. The paper was struggling, like newspapers all did when so many got their news in other ways. "I've been really busy. I'll let you know. Congratulations on your win. I hope you go celebrate. The competition was fierce."

She tried to channel Jessica. Jessica would have no problem saying no if she didn't want to do something. But if she asked for Jessica's advice, she might find out Jessica thought it was a good idea. Sometimes Finn's life could be exhausting.

She was almost to the barn and passed a row of charities seeking donations. That gave her an idea. Instead of focusing on herself, she could use what reach she had to help others. Maybe she would do that interview.

Playing into her own insecurities hadn't benefited anyone, least of all Finn.

Chapter Fourteen

Clint gazed out the window across from his desk, wondering what Finn was doing. The sun was shining brightly in the barn that served as one of the main business offices for Galloway Sons Farm. If she was outdoors, the light would play on Finn's hair, making the red shade even deeper. Clouds like cotton balls drifted in a perfect blue sky, and he let his eyes go half closed.

When would he start sleeping through the night again?

Someone tapped on the exterior door, and Clint's eyes flew open. He straightened in his chair as Gage strode in. Clint's desk was just one of several desks in barn.

Pulling himself to his feet, he greeted his half-brother with a handshake and pat on the arm. "Nice to have you back. We've missed you."

"What're you up to? Not much, from the looks of things."

A tension in Clint's chest flared. He breathed in and it faded. After being here a year, he was proud of himself for learning not to react like a foster kid, not to take offense easily. His brothers didn't mean anything by the little digs they made. It was how they showed brotherly affection and he'd learned the hard way, after hot-headed responses in the early days, which made him stand out. And not in a good way.

"I've been working on a list Wyatt gave me, ordering online for spring. Seed and fertilizer, for starters. We'll be ready to prep the fields for planting. Some machinery's getting prepped too."

Gage went over to the mail area and grabbed some envelopes out of his slot, put one in his front shirt pocket, and sailed the rest into the trash can. "This is your first time here for spring planting, right?"

Clint was excited to be around for spring planting. It helped take his mind off the court date in two days. He walked over toward a storage closet. "It is. I'll help out as I can as we're getting the horse breeding launched."

"I appreciate the update. Hey, I'm going to go take a ride. The weather's great and I'll check out some fences along the way."

"Okay, I cleared out this closet and there's some leftover outdoor apparel and workwear we ordered for the Farm Show. Take anything you need." It sounded silly to his own ears when the guy probably had loads of gear. Maybe he still needed to learn not to try to prove his worth, at times.

Gage grinned. "I sure will. I'm itchin' to get outside. Our place is so beautiful. When I come back after being away, it hits me."

"It's not the same around here without you. Bree and Trey doing okay?"

When Gage and Bree had gotten married, they already had a 5-year-old son, Trey, together. Bree hadn't reached Gage when he worked overseas, so he hadn't known he was a dad when he should have. They'd made it all work in the end.

Would he be able to do that with Finn! Did he want to?

Gage turned toward the door. "They're great. Bree's pregnancy's coming along well. She's feeling good."

The clipped sentences gave Clint the impression he didn't want to talk, loud and clear. Gage shoved open the door and went through.

"Exciting times for you."

Gage was already gone. Some people had everything going

and he was still stuck in a holding pattern. He was happy for the others, though. His time would come. He hoped.

His phone rang and Clint picked up to someone talking. "Yes, this is Clinton F. Galloway."

What was Tate & Tate doing calling him days before court? Couldn't be good news hearing from a lawyer on Monday. "Mr. Tate wants to be sure you have what he's asked for."

"All my character statements are ready, in the format you requested. What else do I need?"

The woman didn't take a breath. "That should do it. Would you be able to bring them to the office or should we send a courier?"

"I'm less than ten miles from town. I'll bring them by in a little while." Their office was on the square. Maybe he would stop over and say hi to Finn while he was in town.

"That would be great. Do you have anything else we can use? School grade reports? Incident reports when the child was with the other custodian. Paternity affidavit?"

Clint went over to his desk and signed out of his computer. "Have you even read my case? I gave you what applied weeks ago. Not tryin' to be rude but a lot's riding on your expertise." He shut the machine down. With any luck, he'd find a reason to be outside the rest of the day.

Clint grabbed his hat and put it on. "The stakes are high. My 15-month-old doesn't have grade reports. She doesn't go to school. I'm the sole custodian. This is my family we're talking about here."

Punching in the code to lock the office door, he headed toward his truck. The grass still had big brown areas but more green showed today than yesterday. "Mr. Galloway, I do apologize. I didn't mean to offend you, and I can assure you we're on top of things. It's a general list we review with everyone. So, we'll see you when you bring the papers."

He hung up just as he rounded the front of his truck, opened the driver's side door, and climbed inside. He powered down every window in the four-door cab all the way down, gunned the motor, removed his hat, and laid it on the seat, just before he pulled away toward town.

He scrolled through his smart phone for the most Hoosier vibe he could find. John Mellencamp's voice filled the cab. He let his hair whip in the wind until he pulled up in front of Hit the Nail. "Not parking in front of a law office. No sense everybody knowing my business," he mumbled to himself.

Bill Tate, Sr. stood beside the receptionist's desk when Clint walked in. Last time, he'd had to wait pretty close to an hour for his appointment. What was up today? They all of a sudden decided to offer customer service along with the bill?

The attorney offered his hand and Clint shook it. The skin was tight and dry, and he couldn't help but compare with Finn's smooth hand. "Are those the character papers?"

Clint nodded. "Every one we discussed, and a few more who volunteered."

He gave the papers to the receptionist. "Please, let's go into my office."

Clint went in and took a seat across from the older man's desk as he sat behind it.

"Thank you for the effort you put into getting people to go on record as character references. It's work but it normally pays off. It can be a good feeling, too, to learn how people support you, even admire what you're doing. Getting sued for custody can be especially painful."

What? Bill Tate had feelings? "I appreciate your saying that. I thought maybe it was just me."

"Clint, I have something else I need to tell you. There's news about Emily. I would typically call in the mother. But the information just came in. Given that Mavis told me you were on your way in to the office, and Ms. Moore signed off on permission for you to receive all communication, I thought I'd share with you."

Clint's mouth went dry. Finn hadn't said anything since she'd taken her signed papers from him weeks ago. He'd hesitated to ask her if she'd turned them in because it wasn't any of his business. She'd listed him as a contact person and he couldn't be more honored. He was caught off guard, too, thinking it'd take months or years to dig up something. "Is her daughter okay?"

"She is. We've found Emily. I didn't know how you wanted to handle this."

Chills ran through Clint. It almost brought him to tears. "Great news. Finn needs to know. What can you tell me? What do we need to do?"

His heart was beating rapidly, almost as fast as when he got word Lilly would be coming to live with him.

Mavis knocked on the door, went over to Clint, and placed a cold bottle of water in his hand.

Her boss didn't skip a beat. "She's in college. And she's studying abroad. I think they will meet in time. Unless you want to make a trip. I'm not sure where exactly, but Finn can find out. I'll put them in contact. Everything's in this folder I'll give you. Please have her call if she has questions. But I'll plan to be in touch when I know more."

* * *

"But I don't want to be called Fiona." Finn looked out the window of Wind in the Willows, dreading the next several minutes. Being called her formal name had always brought out her whining for some reason. She hoped this wouldn't take more than an hour. She gave a side eye toward Jessica.

Jessica sat at her bakery counter and rolled her eyes. "She's going to be here any minute. Just listen to me, okay? I'm not saying people will be calling you Fiona. But for this newspaper story, it sounds good."

"This is why I didn't want to be involved. I knew you'd take over."

Finn's words had barely passed her lips when the overhead bell jingled. She'd been looking for the woman to come from the other direction. Alice from the *Gazette* popped around the corner from their little entry way of plants.

"Hi, girls. Fiona, I hope you're ready for this interview! Do you go by Fiona for purposes of this story?"

"Everyone calls me Finn." She aimed a pointed glare at Jessica. "At least everyone except my bestie. We go back so far, she thinks she knows best."

"Oh, I think Fiona is so pretty for a romantic heroine. I go by Ally, but my professional name is Alice."

"Okay, sounds good then!" No point arguing when she'd been outvoted. She was tired of people voting on things having to do with her, and tamped down how much she wanted to take control of her life from now on.

Younger and more hip than she remembered her being at the essay contest last week, Alice had to be pushing forty, which was years away for Finn. Four whole years. Alice wore her hair in a chic, shorter cut with stylish highlights, and the quick, purposeful way she pulled a slim laptop from her bag radiated energy.

You'd think she'd begun an assignment for a major magazine or something. Well, Finn's business had been growing, so maybe they were both a bigger deal than she first realized.

"Don't give that nice lady a hard time, Finn. People who read newspapers might be the perfect candidates for buying your books."

Alice's confident air stopped Finn from sharing that she'd agreed to this interview mainly because of Jessica. The dilapidated building on Main Street that held the newspaper offices had seen better days. When Finn moved here, everybody said the Fair Creek paper was rumored to be sputtering its last breath. But Alice's essay impressed her and Finn wouldn't count her out yet.

Alice sat on a short stool Finn used so she could shelve higher books in the book shop. "Well, let's get started. I'm on deadline. Oh, why don't I take some photos of you alone, Finn, and as co-businesswomen, with Jessica? I'd like to play up your unique style, how you've combined a bookstore and bakery together like you have here.

"Sounds great. We've agreed that you can emphasize how both our businesses help one another. I owe a lot to Jessica. My bookstore's taken off, basically." Which might be a slight exaggeration but oh well. "She added the hanging sign below her bakery sign you saw out front, sharing equal billing with me. Putting my books in the storefront window along with her tasty baked goods have gotten people in from the street to try both of our temptations."

She never said "tasty," it was like she'd turned into a bad ad.

Alice was typing on her keyboard as fast as she could, which was satisfying somehow.

But where was the woman's camera? Finn automatically ran her fingers through her hair that she'd left flowing down her shoulders. She should have been more prepared and anticipated a photo. But she never really knew how her hair would be anyway so maybe it was just as well. Mascara was her daily go-to so there was that.

Alice fumbled in the pocket of her jeans and pulled out a smart phone. Really? She must have noticed Finn's look of disdain, which was more like a question-mark. "This works just fine for my purposes. The quality's good and I use lots of photos to tell the story, not large ones that might look distorted."

Jessica headed toward the back of her bakery. "I don't need to be in the photo."

"Yes, you do!" Finn and Alice spoke at the same time.

"Oh, okay, I've gotta grab raspberry scones from the oven."

Finn leaned in like she was spilling a secret. "You might want to put in that the bakery side features scones, the British specialty, and Jessica's an expert."

Jessica rushed back in with a tray of the goodies. The aroma was to die for.

Alice hopped off the stool and put her phone and items on it.

"I'd like one. Raspberry scones are from the fruit group, at the least, right?"

Finn pursed her lips and gave Jessica a pleased look as she took the chance to step into the bathroom. Finding her lip gloss in the cabinet, she slathered some on.

Alice had forgotten the photo by the time Finn came back. "Mmmm! Delicious! So, what's new, girl?"

"I'm glad you asked. Since I saw you at the Easter essay contest, I've decided to use the essays as a fundraiser for the town."

Alice looked up from her keyboard. "How do you envision that working?"

Finn walked over to a bookshop and picked up a booklet. "Well, your essay won the top prize, so this won't come as a surprise. Wind in the Willows is going to be selling these essay booklets. The money we raise will go into the Fair Creek funds. It'll go to events like the Fourth of July fireworks, and even next year's Easter egg hunt.'

Alice paused as her next big bite kept her busy chewing.

Finn took charge in the silence. "This'll get my name out, too. I'll explore the idea of offering it online. I'm just not sure. In the next print run, I'll be opening it up to ads. If you want to advertise for the *Gazette*, I'll give you a prime spot."

"That sounds great, I mean, depending on your rates. You did a wonderful job laying out the essays. It'll be almost like the cookbooks churches put together to sell."

Finn hadn't thought about charging for ads, but maybe? Alice could turn out to be a helpful person to share ideas with.

"So what are a couple of types of books that are most popular in your shop?"

Finn took a drink from her go-to water mug. "They're children's books and romance, although I stock cozy mysteries and lots of others, too." She needed to get rid of the romance books somehow. "But there's more. My essay booklets are better than cookbooks. We're going to have the writers read their essays at live events, right here in my shop. It'll be a free will donation kind of thing. Plus, we'll be helping the careers of budding writers."

Finn looked away from Alice just as Clint sprinted by her front window. Her heart skipped a beat, seeing him was so unexpected. Why was he running?

Clueless to her reactions to Clint, Alice forged on. "Oh, speaking of romance, we've heard you're engaged. Wasn't your engagement photo in this very paper a while back?"

"Yep. That was us. I not only came to the country, but I found me a cowboy!"

Clint must have moved his way through the plant jungle, and he burst on the scene at the perfect time.

Finn hopped up and went to him. "What're you doing here?" Had she told him about the interview? She couldn't remember. But she hadn't seen much of him while he prepared for court.

Clint looked at Alice and quirked an eyebrow. He must not have remembered the newspaper reporter or that she was coming. "I've got something important to show you, Finn."

The intensity in his eyes sent some kind of message to her heart.

Jessica had come over by this time. Her best friend looked at the reporter. "She's in the middle of an interview," both women spoke together. They crossed their arms in front of them like nothing else could be more important.

Well, they didn't speak for Finn. Her people-pleasing days were over. "Clint, come with me to the back room so I can see what you have for me." She took his hand and pulled him in the right direction. "Talk among yourselves, you two."

Finn had forgotten how dark it was in the back, especially since she and Jessica kept forgetting to replace the big ceiling light that had blown out. She made an executive decision. "We'll go in here." They went into the bathroom, which was plenty large and had great lighting, what with the big vintage mirror throwing off a reflection.

Clint licked his lips, like his mouth was dry. She couldn't

interpret his expression, but she'd never seen him concentrate so intently. It was almost like she could feel him holding his breath. "I've come from Tate & Tate, you know, the attorneys. Bill Tate gave papers to me for you. I'm sorry you weren't there. He didn't warn me."

This had to be about Emily. Finn's breathing changed. Maybe she was hyperventilating because she was slightly dizzy.

"Let's see if there's a chair for you to sit on. You need to be sitting. . ."

"Give me that." She ripped the little paper thing out of his hand as Clint darted from the bathroom. "Be right back with a stool."

A card on top was typed in bold letters, "Emily Lauren Moore Stover."

Finn's hands started shaking. From the corner of her eye, Clint headed back with the stool. She managed to put the card on the sink. Underneath it was a photo. It was a girl who looked exactly like her.

The room started to spin. She fell and heard a popping noise. Her head throbbed, then everything went black.

Chapter Fifteen

Clint finished snapping Lilly into her pink flowered outfit she'd worn to her first story time. "Remember when you wore this to Finn's book shop?" While sitting on her changing table at home, she could now reach a nearby shelf.

"Bo." She handed Clint a big pink bow from a basket where he kept them.

"Daddy doesn't do bows, honey." Clint denied Lilly nothing, except he couldn't do bows—literally. If he could get them in Lilly's fine hair at all, they always fell out.

"Bo."

That sweet little hand and those big, blue eyes. He sighed. "We'll take your bow with us and see if Aunt Finny can get it to stay, okay?"

"Nn." Her pediatrician said Lilly did well for her age, or at least she would catch up.

He got out her little white knee socks with the lace around the tops he'd left on her changing table. She wiggled, but he managed to get both on. Then he tackled putting on her almost-miniature white sandals.

His phone rang. Its clock said 5 p.m. already. "We better

hustle," he said, then set her on the floor of bedroom before picking up his call.

"Bill Tate here. How are you tonight, Clint?"

He wanted to snap back, "How do you think I'd be the night before our court date?" But he didn't.

He headed over to the bathroom hoping to catch Lilly before she'd undone another roll of toilet paper.

"I know it was a lot with you helping Ms. Moore through opening her adoption. Heard she hit her head in the bookshop bathroom? She okay?"

"She's fine." Get to the point. This was about his little girl and everything else would wait.

"There's more. Louella, as you call her? Her attorney contacted me."

Clint took Lilly's hand and walked her over to see out his window without a curtain. "Yeah, what'd he say?"

"She's dismissed her case. They filed a voluntary discontinuance form."

He sat on his bed and took Lilly in his arms. "Unbelievable. What do you think is going on there? Will she file again?"

"I don't think she will. That's why they called and talked to me, to put your mind at ease. She isn't well and they aren't going into detail for reasons of privacy. But mainly it's because the private investigator didn't find anything on you. They were looking for dirt. But instead, Louella became convinced you're taking excellent care of your daughter, likely better than she could. They're requesting visits, but those would be privately arranged, if they occurred. I would recommend supervised visits only. It's at your discretion."

Bill filled in some details and then their call ended. "Lilly-Bear. Let's go to the party."

Clint started to phone Finn. But such amazing news should be delivered in person. That'd gone so well on Monday. He wanted Lilly to be involved, in whatever ways she could understand. The dismissal would have a big impact on her, which she would learn when she was older.

But for now, he would go on with his plan. "Let's go to Sierra, Wyatt's, and Max's, okay Lilly-Bear?" He didn't know if they'd bring the baby.

When Finn had gotten her news about Emily, Clint had planned a party to celebrate.

His go-to people for family celebrations, Annie and Sierra, had decided to all go to Delaney's tonight. They didn't say it but it was also the night before his court trail. He heaved a sigh of relief he wouldn't have to go.

He pulled the truck up to Wyatt's. Max came out and Wyatt helped him up into the spare car seat next to Lilly. The kids hugged and his heart might be in danger of melting tonight. Seriously.

The Galloway brothers had decided to caravan into town with their families before Clint got the call. They honked and pulled away, reminding him that everything took on an atmosphere of celebration when so many close family members were involved. Once they arrived in Fair Creek, Wyatt came to the truck for Max and took him back with him and Sierra.

Clint and Lilly headed over to Finn's. He'd told her they were going out, and not much more. After tamping down his anticipation at seeing her and sharing his news, the suspense bubbled up as he came closer to being with Finn. He texted her to unlock her outer door into in part of the building, to speed things up.

By the time he knocked on the door of Finn's apartment, Lilly was bright-eyed, like she knew something was up. Most likely, she was feeding off of his vibe.

Finn answered after one knock, not smiling but biting her lip, her shoulders tense. She went out to him in the hallway where he stood and pulled Clint into a hug, with Lilly, too. "What's this all about?"

"What? You don't like a party?" He needed to tell her why he was feeling like a burden was gone.

"Come on in, if you want to. We have time to get to Delaney's, right?"

Lilly broke the ice, flashing Finn her biggest baby grin and shouting her greeting. "Hi!" He stepped into her apartment. The floral sofa and knitted blankets draped over velvety upholstered chairs made him feel instantly at home.

Finn said hi back. And they did another round back and forth.

"We like to share with the whole family when we can. Thanks for clearing your schedule for tonight. How's your head?"

He gingerly touched her bandage covering the bruised lump from her fall in the book shop bathroom.

Lilly frowned. "Boo boo."

"I'm fine. Feeling silly, that's all." Finn wiggled her fingers and Lilly leaned in and went right to her. Finn brought her over to the couch.

"I'm not going to turn down a dinner date with a handsome cowboy and a charming little girl. I hope you weren't worried about rejection."

He smiled and relaxed a little. He held himself back from blurting out his news. "Any headway with connecting with Emily?"

The warmth in her eyes spoke volumes. He'd never seen her so serene, and she hugged Lilly tight. "Clint, we did a video chat."

He swallowed. Maybe the hugs were because something hadn't gone well. "How is she?"

"She's beautiful. Seems sweet, too. We didn't talk long. She had to go to class. We've got time. It happened so quickly because she wanted to meet me. She'd been looking for me."

"That's wonderful. I'm so happy for you. "

She nodded, her eyes shimmering with unshed tears. "It's all thanks to you."

"Oh, no. Well, maybe. Tate sped it along a little."

"I mean talking to you helped me to see I was being too hard on myself. You gave me hope for the future, so I could open my heart to try to find Emily. I'm going to go get something to show you."

She left with Lilly on her hip, and the child's contented expression, patting Finn's back as they went, showed she was happy to be there. In seconds they returned. "This fell out of where I do my readings in the mornings." She showed him a bookmark with a Bible verse on it.

"For I am going to do something in your days that you would not believe even if you were told." Habakkuk 1:5

Clint went over and hugged her. "I didn't dream my life could improve the way it has. Now, I've got to tell you my news. My attorney, our attorney, well, he called. Louella isn't asking for custody anymore. Our court date is cancelled."

"Ohhh." She sat down. "I don't want to risk falling again." She giggled. "This is huge, isn't it, Lilly girl? Thank you, Lord. Guess I can return my courtroom dress I bought."

"Oh, something more fun might come along to wear it for." Clint shared the few details Bill had given him and then it was time to leave for the diner. They bundled in light jackets and walked down the street. As they approached, the streets and lots were all full.

Finn's mouth fell open at all the vehicles. "You have a big family, but this surprises me."

"We've always considered our family to include the Fair Creek community, so we put the word out."

Once inside the restaurant, there were pastel twinkle lights strung along the ceiling. Most tables were full, and in several places, it was standing room only.

When everyone was there, or at least all of those who could fit, Clint called for attention. Finn stood by his side and Lilly held tight around his waist. His little girl didn't like big crowds.

"I've got an announcement. You've all been so kind to Lilly and me since she came to live in Fair Creek. If there's anything we've needed, like advice, or babysitting, or baby food, you've been there. Some of you know I've been in a custody battle for my daughter. That's over and she's staying with me."

The sound of applause filled the room. When things had settled down somewhat, Clint spoke again. "It's a night of fresh starts, and that feels right, with Easter coming up."

Abby stepped forward with Natalie Bogue, the church choir director. "Everybody, we hope you'll come to church Easter Sunday morning," Abby said. "We've got a community choir singing an Easter cantata. If you want to help out and sing, Natalie's offering some private lessons to catch you up. Making a joyful noise is what matters."

As the women made their way back to their people, Cam and Wyatt sauntered up to the front of the room. "We Galloway brothers have buried the hatchet," Wyatt said. "Leo's the boss and he told us to quit it."

That seemed like a good start. Clint held his breath to see what his twin would say.

"Blood is thicker than water." Cam paused for a second or two. "It wasn't my intention to hurt my family and I'm sorry if anyone took offense."

Wyatt pulled his cowboy hat from his head and smashed it on his thigh. "Well, I took offense."

Cam went over to Wyatt and offered his hand, and the two shook hands. "We'll always be brothers, and we don't have to agree on everything."

Each man had a smile on his face, and Clint could breathe again. Wyatt put his arm around Cam's shoulder and his twin followed suit.

This was taking too long and Clint hadn't gotten to the most important part. He moved to the front. "Many of you know Finn and I are engaged. We didn't have an official party, and that's partly what we're doing this evening. You've heard of wedding vow renewal ceremonies? This may be the only engagement vow renewal ceremony ever."

Finn's mouth curved into a smile, and she hugged him and Lilly. "You mean it?" she whispered.

He wanted everyone to hear. "Finn, will you do me the honor of getting engaged all over again?"

"Yes, I will. I want to be with you always." Clint leaned down and kissed her, with Lilly encircled in their embrace. His lips were firm yet tender and conveyed a certainty she felt right down to her toes.

There were more shouts. Then everyone was getting their food and catching up with their neighbors. The Mitchells waved at Finn from a far table.

Kayla walked up and handed Finn a small bouquet. "Congratulations. Had a feeling something good was going to happen tonight."

Finn was putting the flowers in a glass Sierra brought over when Jessica put an arm around Finn. "Hey, glad you didn't let Clint get away. If your plants ever turn on you, he'll know how to save you.'"

Clint came up and took Finn's hand. Lilly's eyes weren't as bright as earlier and he spoke in a quiet tone. "Missed you. Wondered where you went." She nuzzled into his chest for a minute, hearing his heartbeat, which had to be about the best feeling ever.

"Jessica, my brothers and I've only got one more solid day's work and your building's going to be great."

Jessica hugged Finn while Clint continued holding her hand. "How can I ever thank you, both of you?"

When Clint took it upon himself to answer, Finn wondered if he knew Jessica had been rooting for him all along behind the scenes. "Just rememeber, you'll always be family to us. Most of the time, that'll be a good thing. I'll be in touch about the building." He guided Finn away from the crowd, seeming to know just what she needed.

"This has been a blast," she said. "But all I want is to be with you."

Clint found a quiet place to themselves. Lilly'd fallen asleep on his shoulder. "We'll talk more about this when we're really alone. I love you, Finn. I think I always have, since you went along with my fake engagement proposal. I have a confession to make. The only pretending I've been doing these last few weeks is pretending I wasn't falling for you."

He leaned in and their lips met in a kiss she'd never forget, that held the promise of new beginnings. Lilly stirred, and Clint reluctantly pulled away.

Finn thought her heart would overflow. "This is the renewal I wished for that only Easter and spring could bring."

* * *

Continue to enjoy the Galloway Sons Farm series. Cameron Galloway's story is next. He's the new-found brother featured in Her Billionaire Cowboy's Last Chance.

Read on to enjoy how the Galloway Sons Farm Series began with the prequel.

CATHY SHOUSE

HER BILLIONAIRE
COWBOY'S
Twin Heirs

CHRISTMAS IN FAIR CREEK

HER BILLIONAIRE
COWBOY'S
Twin Heirs

★ ★ ★

GALLOWAY SONS FARM
CHRISTMAS IN FAIR CREEK

CATHY SHOUSE

CHAPTER ONE

Annie York peered out the front picture window of Delaney's Diner, wishing the snowflakes would stop. One of the duties of her job was making food deliveries to the surrounding farms and she didn't need slick roads. Indiana weather could be so unpredictable.

With two days until Christmas, Fair Creek shop owners had decorated for the season under their striped green awnings. Hit the Nail hardware had a painted winter scene across the window, and twinkle lights shone on a sixties ornament display at the Vintage Finds antique store. Competition was heating up for the best decorated storefront, with a penny counting for a vote.

If only Annie could get herself into the holiday mood so easily.

"Can you believe your baby turns eight tomorrow?" Sierra Delaney, her cousin and boss, leaned against the counter of the family diner she'd inherited last year. "I couldn't have handled being a mother at eighteen. You've done an amazing job with Chloe."

It didn't seem possible Annie had been a single mom for so

long. "Well, thanks. I was in a haze the first two years or so. Poor kid has a birthday that competes with Christmas week, too."

"Tonight's party will help."

"Thanks for letting me use the diner. I know she put you on the spot by asking."

Sierra glanced out at the street. "It's coming down a little harder. Maybe she'll get her wish for a school snow day on her birthday tomorrow, too."

Annie laughed. "Oh please, don't take her side. Snow would just make my job harder." As an only child, Annie considered her cousin the sister she never had, and also an "aunt" who spoiled Chloe.

Being with Sierra almost made it okay that she'd landed back in Fair Creek after being away for so long. Annie glanced around at the tables and chairs from the eighties in the center of the room and booths on the side to be sure everything was in order.

The old-fashioned wall phone rang, and Sierra picked up. Annie went to get some napkins from the back. When she returned, Sierra was speaking in a stern tone. "You'll just have to hurry back and get them."

Annie continued with her work as Sierra filled her in.

"Hey, that was Brooke. She forgot the pies when she went to cater lunch at Galloway Farm."

Annie tucked away the last bunch of napkins into the dispenser. "She's always forgetting things." Guilt washed over her since she had the same problem as Sierra's part-time college student—focus issues.

Sierra shrugged. "Nobody's perfect. She's good with the customers, but she seemed downright panicked there's not enough time to come back for the pies and fix the meal."

Annie checked her cell phone. "There's plenty of time to make it out to the farm." As much as she hadn't wanted to come back to Fair Creek when she lost her reporter job, she had to keep a roof over their heads, and she jumped at every chance to go out to the country. She'd loved spending time on her grandparents' farm since she was a kid and had been heartbroken when the land had to be sold.

Sierra tucked a piece of her reddish hair back behind her ear. "Maybe we *should* take the pies to the Galloway's."

The bell above the door jingled and Sierra looked up, then waved as a few men who were regulars filed in to their favorite table.

"Nice to see you," her cousin called out.

Ted Mitchell, a retired farmer, tipped his cap with a tractor brand on it. "Don't mind us, just over here solving the world's problems."

He wasn't that far off. In shooting the breeze, as they called it, the buddies had figured out projects and ideas to help the small, tight-knit community, like a piece of new playground equipment at the park or a fundraiser for somebody's house that burned. Sometimes their wives pitched in, too.

Sierra grabbed a cloth and swiped at a spill by the coffeepot. "You sure you don't want me to go out to the Galloways instead of you?"

Annie shook her head. "You were the one who hung around the kitchen and got all the family cooking secrets. I'm not much help here."

"Well, that's not totally true, and you sure gave us some good entertainment on the softball field. But if you're sure, I'll call Brooke back. Hopefully, the snow hasn't gotten too bad. I haven't been able to replace the tires on the van."

While Sierra rang Brooke on her cell, she went over to the work table and motioned for Annie to follow. Annie grabbed her jacket from the hook inside the little office, then had a rhubarb and a black raspberry pie placed into her hands. Both were still warm from the oven. Their sweet scent wafted to her nose as she strode back through the dining room. She leaned one shoulder into the exterior door and shoved it open, pressing against the Santa face that Chloe had painted on the glass.

A shot of brisk air greeted her, and her sneakers grabbed for stability on the sidewalk glazed with snow. A glance at the snow coming down lifted her spirits because it was so pretty, like wrapping the town in the magic of Christmas.

Chloe's birthday always reminded Annie that another year had passed and Chloe was still an only child. When Annie was a little girl, she had desperately wanted a brother or sister, vowing that if she ever was a mother, she'd have at least two children. Yet at twenty-six, and in her financial straits, Annie had no prospects and couldn't afford to adopt.

She glanced at The Lone Mum florist shop window down the street, with a lighted mom, dad, and baby reindeer grazing beside a vintage red barn under the Christmas Star. If only that could be real, because as much as they loved being a team of two, Chloe would like others to be added. Annie and Chloe had put all their penny votes into the jar at that display.

Something slammed into her legs, a soft yet solid mass of motion. Annie lost her balance, began to fall, and tried to catch herself. But the rhubarb pie sailed away and landed with a scrape of foil onto the sidewalk.

Her knees smacked against the cement. She winced as pain radiated around the joints but somehow the raspberry pie stayed in her hand, unharmed.

Heavy footsteps resonated from somewhere, coming closer. "Bentley!" A male voice cut through her confusion. An overgrown black-and-white dog stood near her feet and cocked its head to one side. Then he trotted to Annie's smashed pie, sniffing at the filling that oozed onto the sidewalk.

"Are you all right? Let me help." The man looking down from under the cowboy hat had wavy, coal-black hair and his jeans fit his muscular body, likely honed by physical labor of some type. The man defined hunk, and his voice reverberated somewhere deep in his chest. A shiver darted up Annie's spine.

No man had made that happen in a while. Maybe ever.

Annie took a mental inventory and nothing seemed seriously wrong. Good, since showing she was hurt was the last thing she wanted. She'd learned as a single mom that she couldn't depend on anybody.

"I'm fine. Surprised, mainly." She glanced at the dog. "That pie took a hit."

The man hunched down, holding a leash in one hand, and offering her the other.

She waved him away, still feeling a bit jostled. Without realizing, her grip tightened and her thumb poked a dent into the crust of her one remaining pie.

"Really, no harm done." She was always reassuring people she was fine, and it got old. What would it be like to have someone who watched out for her and picked her up when she needed it?

The man stood to his full height, his arm still extended toward her. "Please, let me."

If it would make him feel better. She handed him the pie and their fingers brushed. The warmth of his touch made her breath catch.

Startled, she pulled away, making a production of dusting off her jeans. She really was okay, except for some stinging pain where her knees and hand had connected with the ground.

"I'm Caleb." He paused, like he was going to say something and then changed his mind. "Bentley's a good dog, just excitable."

She batted his hand away. "I'll say." She pointedly glanced at Bentley wolfing down the pie on the sidewalk and winced. "Keep that brute away from me."

She could have been hurt badly, and it might have been far worse if the dog had run into a small child or one of the older men inside the diner.

"I'll make it up to you."

"I've heard that a few times before. I don't know where you come from, but we have leash laws."

"I'm not from around here. At least, not anymore." His dark brown eyes had a playful spark as his gaze met hers.

She had to admit, everything about the man appealed to her. He had an easy smile with nearly perfect teeth and a dimple. She never noticed things like that. There was just something about him, and Annie found herself questioning whether being a single mother really was all God had in mind for her.

Pushing a wisp of hair from her eyes, she opted not to confess her weakness for guys in cowboy hats. She saw them all day long, but he won the award for most handsome.

Hopefully, he didn't notice her blushing. The man looked familiar, but with that jawline, she'd surely remember if they'd met. Not that finding a man was on her radar. She'd thought herself in love once, and that had been enough. Chloe came first, ahead of any crazy hormone reaction. The last thing she needed was a major distraction in her life, with so many minor ones already.

Bentley barked at the empty pie pan, then came to Caleb, who managed to snap on his leash while hanging onto the pie Annie had given him.

Caleb shrugged. "He's Dad's dog. I haven't been home long enough to get to know him."

Caleb looked toward the only vehicle Annie didn't recognize on the street, a huge, shiny-red pick-up truck parked at the curb.

"He was supposed to stay in the truck bed."

"Whatever. I'm not letting that cute face fool me."

And that applied to the man *and* the dog.

The snow was really coming down, and a little way up the street, the Delaney's Diner van with its bald tires looked like an even worse excuse for transportation. But she concentrated on avoiding this man's intense eyes. Definitely wanted to ignore the way his T-shirt covered his chest and strained against the fabric, peeking from underneath his woolly lined jacket.

With her good, non-scraped-up hand, Annie wrenched her phone from her jeans pocket. Eleven o'clock. She could still make it.

"I'm on a delivery run to Galloway Farm." Taking the pie back from him, she was careful they didn't touch.

His cocoa-colored eyes deepened. "We're heading to the same place." The corners of his mouth tipped up.

In spite of herself, Annie smiled and inhaled, bringing a calmness and easing the tension in her shoulders. She glanced at the damaged pie, which would do for her and Chloe later, then turned to go back inside the diner for replacement pies. She swayed slightly, and a strong, muscular arm came around her. She couldn't resist leaning into his scent, a mix of soap and pricey aftershave, and lingered a bit longer than necessary. Finally, she steadied herself and stepped away.

Wait, if he was headed to the Galloway Farm.... "You're Caleb Galloway." Just her luck, Caleb Galloway had grown up to be gorgeous.

He'd been a scrawny, computer geek a couple of grades above her in high school and had borne no resemblance to his family. Except standing before her now, his tall, noble features and good looks resembled cowboys in the movies.

With the back of his hand, he grazed the stubble along his chin. "It took me a minute, too, Annie York." Caleb looked her over with an unreadable expression on his well-bred face. "You wrote for the school paper and played sports, didn't you?"

"The good old days."

"It's great to see you again." He emphasized the words, like he meant it. "Too bad it wasn't a gentler reunion. Dogs will be dogs, I guess."

"Look, you can dogsplain all you want. But I'm lucky to be alive."

He chuckled. "Maybe I missed something. Were you in the drama club?"

His playful tone broke down her resistance. She let a smile show. "Easy for you. Your life didn't pass before your eyes."

As she headed into Delaney's, he walked with her. For once, it was nice to feel protected.

She collected two fresh pies and went out to the sidewalk again. The snow had started to build up on the sidewalk. Caleb looked in the direction of Galloway Farms. "There are some hairpin turns on the roads getting to our family's property. I'd feel a whole lot better if you'd let me drive you."

"Oh, that won't be necessary." The snow did worry her, but he didn't need to know that.

He pointed at Sierra's old van, which was hard to miss with the Delaney's Diner logo and messages all over it.

"That isn't going to get a lot of traction in snow. You don't welcome my help, but I'm the reason you're late. We're going in the same direction, and I have the time to bring you back."

"I appreciate it. But none of this was really your fault. I mean, other than the dog and the ruined pies." She grinned. Something in her wanted to ride in his big fancy truck, but she knew from experience that she'd do better to let sleeping dogs lie and not get involved.

She couldn't believe the words that came out of her mouth next. "Well, why don't you take one of these pies and help me up into the cab of your truck?"

CHAPTER TWO

Caleb nudged the gas pedal with care as he parked his dad's extended cab pick-up by the barn. His sports car at home in L.A. handled differently and he didn't want to ding the old man's pride and joy. Annie York sat perched on the passenger side of the truck's bench seat, and keeping his mind on driving was proving a challenge. But that was nothing compared to how hard it had been to convince her to let him drive her. It hurt his pride a little, but he didn't claim to understand women. Usually, it wasn't much work to get them to spend time with him.

He appreciated having her as a distraction. Things on the farm hadn't been so run down the last time he was here. With the snowfall, he couldn't see past two large horse barns with slightly sagging roofs and a training area with a fence with slats loose, but he knew that everything called for a fresh coat of paint at the bare minimum. Mom's big decorated wreath at the barn's peak, which she had hung every Christmas, should have cheered him, but it only reminded him of better days. He swallowed.

He sneaked a peek at Annie. They'd driven from town with his focus mainly on the snowy road, and the radio blaring with music from their school days. He liked how some wisps of her hair escaped her ponytail and accentuated the delicate nape of her neck. Her beauty caught him up short as she seemed occupied with looking straight out the windshield. Couldn't blame her if there wasn't much conversation. The wholesome Indiana look he remembered, of blond hair, blue eyes, and athletic build was there, but now she was filled out with a woman's curves that added to her appeal. She was muscular and wouldn't blow away in the wind, something he'd always found attractive. They hadn't known one another well, but he'd admired her from afar. He wasn't sure if her stubborn streak was new, but he found her intriguing—more determined to take care of herself than other women he'd met.

Caleb shut off the truck.

Annie shifted her gaze out the side window, seeming to look past the barns to the fields. "The beauty of this place…"

"You've been here before?" The family farm had never attracted him and certainly didn't now. Since he was a young boy, he'd fought the pull of the land and couldn't get away fast enough.

"Since your mom passed—and I'm really sorry for your loss— the diner has helped out a lot with food. I always appreciate the chance to come here."

Really. Annie would be one good reason to spend more time here. If the only one.

What had gotten into him? He lifted his hat, smoothed his hair underneath, and replaced the borrowed Stetson. Maybe turning thirty soon was messing with his head.

He unpacked himself from behind the steering wheel and let down the tailgate. Bentley bounded out and went off on some rabbit trail. After going around to open the cab door, he helped Annie down, and they each took a pie. Going over the rough ground to the ranch house concerned him, since Bentley had done a number on Annie earlier and he wasn't sure if she was fully okay.

"There are some uneven places," he said. "If you lean on me without arguing, I'll share my piece of pie."

Her smile, sweet and sassy at the same time, spread so big it reached into his heart. "Deal. Black raspberry's my favorite."

He lowered his elbow, and she latched on. The fruity scent of her hair enticed him and he enjoyed the closeness.

Whoa. Women were off his agenda. He'd learned the hard way women were only interested in one thing—his bank account. He did have a fortune, earned all on his own.

The back door sprang open, pushed hard from within, and Caleb leaned toward Annie, to protect her from whatever came next.

"What kept you?" Dad's face showed all of his years and then some, his expression like a rain cloud as he ushered them inside.

Caleb frowned as Dad held the door for them to come in. "Didn't know there was any hurry. I brought Annie since she needed to bring pies and the weather's not great on the side roads."

The response was a grumble and a gesture toward the other end of the room. Dad was always on edge these days, trying to keep the farm going. But Caleb expected a better greeting for his guest. He shrugged, trying to shake his annoyance.

The big old farmhouse kitchen would always be his mother's, and he could almost see her standing there by the stove making mashed potatoes and gravy, his favorite, like she'd always done. Oak cabinets lined the walls, still full of all of her things, he was sure, and the room smelled of fried chicken and other foods he couldn't name. But now everything had been prepared by others. He swallowed a lump in his throat. Had it really been two years? They used to talk almost every day. Caleb removed his hat and Annie carried the pies to the young woman at the counter who also worked at Delaney's, as she had explained on the way over.

Someone he'd never seen before sat in a chair with her arms wrapped around two lookalike babies in snowsuits that had been unzipped—one in pink, and the other in pale blue. Their heads were covered in red stocking caps with a soft-looking, white pompom ball on the end, each like a junior Santa's helper.

"Excuse me for not standing, Caleb. I'm Lorraine Landry from Child Protective Services. These are your sister's twins. Meet Drew and Ella. You're listed as their guardian. Before we continue, would you please show me a form of legal I.D. so I know I'm speaking with the correct person?"

There must be some mistake. He reached for his wallet.

He was no one's guardian, except maybe Bentley's. And look how well that was going. He handed her his driver's license, two sets of little eyes watching his every move. They were adorable babies and he hadn't seen them since right after they were born.

To her credit, Ms. Landry recognized his inability to find words and filled in the silence, after returning his license to him. "Their mom, your sister Kayla, is in rehab for opioid addiction."

Caleb swallowed. Out of the corner of his eye, Dad sank hard into a chair by the table. He was still near enough to overhear the conversation while three farm hands finished their noon meal with him, although he wasn't eating a bite. In his peripheral vision, Annie and her helper seemed to be hovering over their work, not talking to each other, probably listening in on his predicament.

"Kayla called me a while back, said things were going better," he said.

The Landry woman's expression turned solemn, not that she'd been smiling before. "That's the nature of addiction. Ups and downs."

Caleb's chest tightened. His little sister had been estranged from the family until that first call from out of the blue after the babies were born. She'd wanted him to sign some papers. It was the only thing she'd ever asked of him since they were kids. Back then she'd followed him everywhere, always wanting ice cream and to be just like him. How could he refuse?

He swiped his arm across his brow as he started to perspire. But he purposely tried to sound casual. "Where's their daddy?"

She shook her head from side to side, the motion reeking with disapproval. "In worse shape than Kayla is." The baby girl craned her neck toward Caleb, innocent brown eyes searching his face, almost like she understood she was the topic of conversation. Caleb got up and paced around the room.

When he got in front of the babies, he picked up the little guy, hefty-looking yet light as a feather. "I was your back-up guardian. Never really thought it'd come to this..."

Could a person apologize to a baby and have them understand?

The big brown eyes looked directly into his, then the little hand reached over and patted his shoulder two times. His heart melted under the gentle touch.

The day Caleb signed the papers, his sister made sure to introduce them properly in person. They sure had grown. Some unidentified sweet scent wafted up from the little head. His chin grazed the cap and a stray tuft of baby-fine hair brushed his neck.

Don't get too attached to them, Caleb. You're definitely not dad material.

John Galloway rested both of his hands on the oak table. "Miss Landry, my son can't manage these babies."

Guilt washed over Caleb. He had only been thinking about his own situation. Dad had a falling out with Kayla years ago. She'd stolen from him for drugs, which started the estrangement.

A kind, gentle voice broke into his thoughts. Annie directed a question to Lorraine. "She's beautiful. May I hold her?"

Not waiting for a response, Annie hunched down at eye level to the dark-haired baby, her fingers outstretched. "Will you come to me, Ella?"

The baby leaned forward and launched herself into Annie's outstretched arms.

Caleb's heart tilted and he gave Drew a slight squeeze. Ella and Drew were living, breathing babies who deserved better. His family's own flesh and blood. "Dad, I made a commitment. I intend to keep it." He let the anguish show in his voice. "I didn't think I'd ever be called on. You have to believe me. We can't let someone else..." He choked up slightly, and he was sure his face was flushed.

Annie gathered Drew from his arms. Babies on each hip, she carried them to an angel suncatcher, it's bright golden halo decorated with a small Christmas wreath, that was attached to the window over the sink. "I heard a story once that your grandma collected angels," Annie said. Each baby's tiny fingers reached for the hanging ornament and made the doodad sway.

The way she talked to his niece and nephew registered deeply. He needed to man up, starting now. "Whatever I need to do to get the ball rolling..."

A wooden chair scraped on the linoleum and Dad left the room. In a daze, Caleb signed the papers. He reached for the bag and car seats on the floor next to Lorraine. "I'm not really set up for one baby, let alone two of them. You've caught me off guard."

The woman nodded and didn't smile. "You'll be surprised how quickly caring for them becomes routine. A lovely connection, even."

Caleb's stomach growled, but not from hunger.

Food. What did a baby eat?

"What do I feed them and how much?" He had asked those questions when he got Bentley, but now they seemed inadequate and not for babies. What were their favorite foods? Did they even eat solid food yet? Did they like to be rocked?

"Instructions in the bag, with formula and bottles. Like every parent, you'll adapt. Soon you'll be wondering how you ever did without these sweeties. And don't worry, we'll be following up."

Just what he didn't want to hear, since he had no idea how the three of them would survive the weekend, let alone longer. "Wait. How long is this going to last?"

"Wish I knew, but it's hard to say. Better plan on having them for a while."

Caleb swallowed. Surely Kayla could help some? "Can they see their mom?"

"No visits. If anything changes, we'll let you know. You're doing something wonderful. You'll see."

Annie stepped up and smiled at Caleb. His niece nestled deeper into her neck, eyes drooping. "I need to get back to town. Chloe, my eight-year-old, is in school today and gets out in a couple hours," she said. "I mean, she's got a play date after but I like to be in the area, in case signals got crossed or something."

Caleb inhaled. Annie had a daughter. That shouldn't matter to him, but it did somehow. She would have told him if she was married. Was the dad in the picture? He went over to the counter and picked up his hat. Why did he care if there was a man in Annie's life? No wonder she looked so natural.

So that's why she knew what she was doing.

Annie talked without stopping, like she might be concerned about his reaction. "Why don't you and the babies come to our place until you figure things out? Maybe I can give you some baby lessons. Small stuff, about pacifiers and naptime, can make all the difference."

She might be the only lifeline he had. "I don't want to put you out. They're my responsibility, uh, but if you wouldn't mind..." Dad needed space, and it wasn't fair to have them here when he was so upset.

Annie laughed and kissed each baby's cheek. "Between the two of us, they'll survive. So let me pack that piece of pie, or four. Comfort food."

She grinned and he felt the warmth deep down. Not a welcome sign, because spending time with her might loosen his resolve to keep his distance from women. Pie sounded good, though. He welcomed a sugary dessert, especially now, with his mind overloaded with questions.

What was he going to do? What else could possibly go wrong?

The only thing that seemed to be going right was Annie, and that was his biggest concern next to these babies.

Read More By

CATHY SHOUSE

Her Billionaire Cowboy's Twin Heirs: Christmas in Fair Creek (A Fair Creek Romance, prequel)

Her Billionaire Cowboy's Second Chance: Galloway Sons Farm (A Fair Creek Romance, Book 1)

Her Billionaire Cowboy's Triplets: Galloway Sons Farm (Christmas in Fair Creek, Book 2)

Her Billionaire Cowboy's Best Friend: Galloway Sons Farm (A Fair Creek Romance, Book 3)

Her Billionaire Cowboy's Secret Heir: Galloway Sons Farm (Christmas in Fair Creek, Book 4)

Her Billionaire Cowboy's Pretend Proposal: Galloway Sons Farm (A Fair Creek Romance, Book 5)

Her Billionaire Cowboy's Last Chance: Galloway Sons Farm (A Fair Creek Romance, Book 6)

About

CATHY SHOUSE

Cathy Shouse writes inspirational cowboy romance. Her Fair Creek series, set in Indiana, features the Galloway brothers of Galloway Sons Farm. Much like the characters in her stories, Cathy once lived on a farm in "small town" Indiana where she first fell in love with cowboys while visiting the rodeo every summer.

Sign up to receive her newsletter at: www.cathyshouse.com where you'll get free books, exclusive bonus content, and news of her releases and sales.

If you liked this book, please take a moment to review it! Authors (including Cathy) really appreciate this, and it helps draw more readers to books they might like. Thanks!